YA
Kee
pb

EXPLOSIVE SITUATION

Standing in the woods, close to the waterfront, Joe searched the sea with his binoculars. He noticed one barge moving slowly closer to the wooded coast—straight toward the spot where the two trucks were hidden.

Moving as quietly as he could, Joe crept closer to the spot where the trucks were. He was still a couple of hundred feet from them, but by the time the barge got to the coast he'd be in perfect position to observe. Every instinct in his body told him that the stolen Phoenix missiles were on that barge.

You've got the magic touch, no doubt about it, Joe congratulated himself. We've been here less than a day, and you've almost cracked this case wide op—

Ka-blam!

A deafening explosion rocked the entire peninsula, sending Joe diving for cover. He threw one arm over his head and quickly grabbed his binoculars with the other. He put them to his eyes. Huge flames rose up from the trucks' metal cabs, licking at the branches of the nearby trees. . . .

Nancy Drew & Hardy Boys SuperMysteries

Available from ARCHWAY Paperbacks

A NANCY DREW AND HARDY BOYS SUPER MYSTERY™

ISLANDS OF INTRIGUE

Carolyn Keene

AN ARCHWAY PAPERBACK
Published by POCKET BOOKS
New York London Toronto Sydney Tokyo Singapore

AN ARCHWAY PAPERBACK *Original*

 An Archway Paperback published by
POCKET BOOKS, a division of Simon & Schuster Inc.
1230 Avenue of the Americas, New York, NY 10020

Copyright © 1996 by Simon & Schuster Inc.
Produced by Mega-Books, Inc.

ISBN: 0-671-50294-8

First Archway Paperback printing May 1996

10 9 8 7 6 5 4 3 2 1

NANCY DREW, THE HARDY BOYS, AN ARCHWAY PAPERBACK and colophon are registered trademarks of Simon & Schuster Inc.

A NANCY DREW AND HARDY BOYS SUPERMYSTERY is a trademark of Simon & Schuster Inc.

Cover art by Brian Kotzky

Printed in the U.S.A.

IL 6+

Chapter

One

"SO THIS IS THE CRADLE of Western civilization, huh?" Joe Hardy asked.

Frank Hardy stopped next to his brother on the hot, crowded sidewalk in Athens, Greece. He could see the classical marble columns of the Acropolis, way up on a hill overlooking Athens. But here in the middle of the city, most of the buildings were modern, boxlike structures of stuccoed cement. Chattering tourists filled the cafés lining Syntagma Square, and horns blared from the cars, trucks, and motorcycles that swarmed past.

"Not exactly the kind of place where you'd imagine ancient Greek philosophers hanging out and debating the meaning of life," Frank said, cracking a smile. "But I guess the Gray Man didn't send us here so we could catch up on history."

1

"You got *that* right." Joe looked left and right around the crowded square, tapping his sneaker on the sidewalk. "Where's the kiosk where we're supposed to make contact?"

"Let's see. Southeast corner of Syntagma Square," Frank said as he recalled the Gray Man's instructions, then checked his pocket map. "It should be right around here . . . somewhere. . . ."

When the Gray Man had called to ask if they'd help him—unofficially, of course—with a mission, he'd warned them that it would be dangerous. He hadn't given them many details—just that they'd be helping to recover some missiles stolen from a U.S. military base near Athens. All of the background information would be handed to them by an agent posing as a vendor at a newsstand.

"Bingo." Joe pointed to a small, octagonal structure about fifty feet in front of them. Behind the racks of newspapers and magazines stood an older man with wiry gray hair and a stubble of unshaved beard.

"Here goes," Frank said under his breath. Shoving his hands in his jeans pockets, he sauntered over to the stand and checked out the newspapers. "Excuse me," he said, repeating the code words precisely. "I'm looking for a map of the Dodecanese islands."

The man's alert gaze flicked over Frank's face

before he spoke. "Is there a particular island you'd like to travel to?" the vendor asked.

So far, so good. That was exactly the response the Gray Man had told Frank to expect. "Rhodes," Frank told the man. Then he lowered his voice and added, "I've heard the figs are excellent there."

The vendor gave a crisp nod. Reaching under the counter, he pulled out a flat package wrapped in brown paper. On top of the package was a folded-up map. Frank felt a rush of adrenaline as he tucked the package under his arm and crossed back to Joe. "Come on. Let's find someplace where we can look this over."

As the two crossed a street, Frank spotted a large public garden with paths cutting neatly among well-trimmed lawns and flowers.

"There's a bench under that tree over there," Joe said, pointing to a deserted spot.

As soon as they sat down, Frank unwrapped the package. Inside was a manila folder filled with photographs, articles, and classified background material on the case. Frank and Joe quickly scanned the cover sheet.

"Whoa!" Joe said. He leaned back on the bench and let out a low whistle. "No wonder the Gray Man warned us that this job would be tough. I mean, tracking down one of our own undercover operatives *and* a half-dozen Phoenix missiles he's suspected of stealing?"

Frank could hardly believe it himself. According to the cover sheet, it was a case of a good agent gone bad. Terry Brodsky had been the top U.S. undercover man in the Balkans for the past five years. Missions took him all over the area, but his home base was the one near Athens where the Phoenix missiles had been stored. Brodsky had dropped out of sight at the same time that the missiles were stolen. Since Brodsky knew all the network's undercover operatives, the Gray Man had brought in Frank and Joe to help track Brodsky because he wouldn't know them.

Frank flipped to the second sheet, which gave background information on Brodsky. "Check out his record. He's the guy who infiltrated that terrorist group in the Mideast a few years back and recovered six American hostages," he told Joe. "A weapons expert . . . top security clearance . . ."

"Hmm," Joe said, reading over Frank's shoulder. "His latest mission was to set up a deal to sell U.S. arms to Petronia."

Frank vaguely remembered reading about negotiations between the U.S. and Petronia, a tiny Balkan nation. Petronia was to acquire U.S. technology after its military government was replaced by a democracy. "The sale fell through because of an international arms reduction treaty."

"Yup," Joe said. "Anyway, it looks like the one

4

complaint the top brass had about Brodsky was that he didn't play by the rules."

While Joe spoke, Frank scanned another memo in the file on his lap. "Which apparently didn't go over very well with the guy who wrote this," he said, showing the memo to Joe. "General Warren Blackman, who's the new director of undercover forces in the Balkans, is the kind of guy who does everything strictly by the book. He wrote this to his commanding officer back in the States, recommending that Brodsky be removed because of his 'unorthodox methods.'"

"Brodsky went a lot further than bending the rules this time," Joe said. "Six Phoenix missiles and Brodsky all disappear at the same time. What are we supposed to think, that he suddenly took a vacation?"

"Yeah, right. And he happened to forget to tell everyone about it," Frank scoffed. "If you ask me, stealing the missiles was Brodsky's way of leaving the undercover forces before getting kicked out. The cover sheet mentions a photo that implicates Brodsky, too, doesn't it?"

Joe flipped through to some photographs at the back of the file. "It must be one of these," he said, handing the stack to Frank.

The top photo was a shot of Terry Brodsky from the Pentagon's personnel files. Frank studied it closely. The man staring out at him had piercing blue eyes, sandy hair, and a rugged, angular face. His powerful build was evident, even beneath his button-down shirt. "Not the kind of guy you'd want to run into in a deserted alley," Frank said.

"No kidding." Joe plucked two more photos from the pile in Frank's hands, then turned one over. "It says here on the back that this picture was sent by an anonymous source. It's the kind that has the date and time automatically printed on it. Looks like it was taken the night the missiles were stolen. One's the original. The other's a computer enhancement."

Frank peered at the photo. "It was sent anonymously, so it's not completely reliable, but it is pretty incriminating."

The original photo was dark and blurred. All Frank could make out was the boxy black silhouette of a truck and the shadowy figure of a man next to it. The computer enhancement showed what looked like missiles inside the truck. The details of the man's face were much clearer, too. There was no mistaking Brodsky's angular features.

"The cover info said something about a military truck being found abandoned outside of Athens," Frank said. "So maybe the missiles are somewhere around here."

Joe nodded, scanning the cover sheet. "It's pretty obvious that Petronia was disappointed when the arms sale didn't go through. Since Brodsky *was* in on the negotiations . . ."

"Maybe he's selling the stolen missiles to Petronia on his own," Frank finished. "With the money he'd get, Brodsky could start a new life for himself anywhere he wants—unless we stop him."

"The question is, how?" Joe asked. "This background sheet says that agents have been monitoring all trucks and ships crossing into Petronia. So far, nothing's turned up except that one abandoned truck. The Gray Man thinks Brodsky may be hiding the missiles somewhere near Athens until the heat dies down."

"Or, if the deal with Petronia isn't firm yet, Brodsky might have to stay put here until everything's worked out," Frank put in.

There were two photographs remaining in the pile—one was of a slender man with balding dark hair, shaking Terry Brodsky's hand. "This was taken while the arms negotiations were still on," Frank said, after checking the description on the back of the photo. "This guy, Dvorniak, is the Petronian ambassador to Greece. He's definitely someone to keep an eye on. If an illegal deal is going down, he could be Brodsky's contact."

The other photograph showed a man with short dark hair and an impeccably trimmed beard. "Here's suspect number two, Josef Kozani," Frank went on. "Officially, he's a Petronian businessman. He's got an international reputation as a consultant."

"He's the guy who convinced U.S. businesses to invest in Petronia after they became a democracy in the late 1980s, right?" Joe said. He raised an eyebrow at Frank. "Let me guess. He has a sideline dealing in illegal weapons?"

Frank checked the background sheet attached to Kozani's photograph. "That's what the Pentagon thinks. Apparently, he's been suspected of being involved in other illegal arms deals, though nothing has ever been proven," he said. "We should probably check the main hotels to see if he's in Athens."

"Let's get something to eat first, okay?" Joe suggested.

"Sounds good," Frank agreed. "I'm starved." He flipped the file shut and got to his feet. "We can probably get some souvlaki at one of the cafés on Syntagma Square."

"Souvlaki?" Joe echoed as they left the gardens and headed back to the crowded square. "What's that?"

He broke off and elbowed Frank in the ribs. "I don't believe it," he said, dropping his voice to a low whisper. "Check out who's right in front of us."

He was staring at a man in a gray business suit. "Josef Kozani!" Frank whispered. "Keep cool. We don't want him to get suspicious."

The Hardys hung back, letting Kozani take a comfortable lead. Then they followed him right onto a street called Vasilissis Sofias. Frank noticed the different national flags on the ornate buildings they passed.

"Looks like there are a lot of embassies here." Frank took his map of Athens from his back pocket.

"Even Petronia's?" Joe asked doubtfully.

"Why not? Petronia *does* border Greece to the north," Frank said as he studied the map. "The map says it's here." He pointed to a spot on the map, then shot Joe a meaningful glance. "The embassy's only a few blocks away."

Up ahead, Josef Kozani was turning left onto a side street. The narrow street was lined with stores and restaurants. About halfway down, Kozani crossed the street and entered a café. A sign over the door read Taverna Salamandra, above the Greek symbols.

"Definitely not the embassy," Joe said, staring at the taverna. "Maybe he's got some sort of rendezvous."

"Or maybe he's just having lunch," Frank reminded his brother. "It could be a total coincidence that he's in this area."

"Well . . ." Joe squared his shoulders and started across the street. "Let's find out."

Frank had already started to follow his brother, when he heard the whining buzz of a moped somewhere off to their left. He turned his head—then froze.

A red moped was barreling down the narrow street at top speed, and it was heading straight for him and Joe.

"Stop!" he cried, but the driver didn't even slow down or swerve. In a second the moped was going to be on top of them!

Chapter

Two

J OE WHIPPED HIS HEAD around and saw the red moped. He caught a glimpse of long, dark hair and sunlight glinting off a helmet but had no time to react.

"Hey!" Joe felt his feet fly out from under him as Frank hit him in a full tackle. They both went soaring, and a second later Joe's right shoulder hit the pavement with a painful crack. Then came the searing heat as the moped whizzed past just inches from his head. It was so loud that Joe felt as if someone had turned a lawn mower on inside his brain. Finally the noise faded and he heard Frank's voice right next to him.

"You okay, Joe?"

Joe blinked, trying to catch his breath. Frank was crouched next to him, peering at him expectantly. Papers and photographs were strewn all over the street and sidewalk. Frank must have dropped the background material, Joe thought, when he tackled him.

"Fine," Joe gasped out. "Couldn't be better."

With a groan, he pushed himself to a sitting position and rubbed his shoulder. Then he unzipped his belt pack and checked it. Before leaving their youth hostel that day, he'd stowed binoculars and a lock-picking set in the pack. Luckily, neither appeared to be damaged.

"Ever consider a career in the NFL, Frank?" he asked. "I'm no talent scout, but I'd say you show a lot of promise."

"And give up the glamour of high school?" Frank grinned, rubbing at a greasy stain on his T-shirt. "Never."

Joe shook his head and grabbed a handful of papers. "Yeah, you're right. Come on. Let's pick this stuff up before—"

He cut himself off in midsentence to peer down the street. The sound of a moped's engine was growing louder. "Not again," Joe groaned. He tensed when the red moped appeared from a side street. This time, at least, it was going slowly. The driver was a girl, he saw. She stopped a few feet from him and Frank and began to unstrap her helmet. She started to say something, but Frank cut her off.

"Sorry, but my brother and I don't speak Greek," he said. He swept up a few more papers from the street and handed them to Joe.

"Besides, we're kind of busy here," Joe added.

He shot Frank a meaningful look, then nodded to the café where Josef Kozani had gone. "Frank, don't you, uh, need to use the phone in there?" He didn't know if the girl spoke any English, but he figured it would be better not to let on that they were following Kozani.

"Definitely. Back in a flash." Frank gave him a nod before jogging over to the taverna and disappearing inside.

"You are American?" the young woman asked in a lightly accented voice.

Joe turned to look at her and then did a double-take. He'd been so busy picking up papers from the file that he hadn't noticed her sparkling brown eyes, or the way her long, wavy black hair spilled carelessly over her shoulders. Talk about a total knockout! The girl appeared to be a couple of years older than he and Frank, maybe twenty. She was petite and curvy, and there was something irresistibly impish about her.

Shooting the girl a wide grin, Joe held out his hand and said, "Hi, there. I'm Joe Hardy. My brother, Frank, and I are visiting from the States."

"My name is Sofia Alcalay," she told him. "I am very sorry about what happened. I did not see you until it was too late to stop. You are hurt?"

"Nah," he said, ignoring his aching shoulder. A hot breeze gusted down the narrow street, stirring the last few papers and photos. Joe jumped to retrieve them. When Sofia bent to help him, he tried to stop her, but it was too late.

"Josef Kozani!" Sofia exclaimed, staring in surprise at the photograph of the businessman as she picked it up. "He is a hero in my country."

Joe looked at Sofia in surprise. "You're not Greek?" he asked.

She shook her head. "I am a student at Athens University, but my native country is Petronia."

Just then Frank came out of the taverna. As he walked back over to Joe and Sofia, he frowned and gave an imperceptible shake of his head. Joe got the message: Kozani had gotten away.

"Sofia Alcalay, meet my brother, Frank Hardy," Joe said. He raised an eyebrow at Frank before adding, "Sofia's from Petronia," Joe said.

"Oh, yeah?" Frank asked, his eyes narrowing.

"Yes." Sofia smiled at him, then pointed to the photo of Kozani. "I did not think that most Americans knew about our greatest business leader."

Joe caught the expression of dismay that flashed across his brother's face. Whatever else happened, they couldn't risk her finding out the true reason for their trip to Athens. "Yeah, well, Frank and I are journalists," Joe fibbed, smoothly taking the photograph from Sofia. "One of the reasons we're in Athens is to, uh, try to interview Kozani for a story we're doing on him."

"Really?" Sofia's brown eyes sparkled with interest as she stepped closer to Joe. "I am writing my thesis at the university on Mr. Kozani's methods of attracting foreign business to Petronia. More than anything, I would like to interview him. But . . ." She let out a sigh. "So far I have not been successful."

Joe caught the warning Frank shot him. "We really can't—" Frank began, but Joe cut him off.

"We'll be glad to help you out if we can," he said, giving Sofia another winning smile. "I mean, a guy as famous as Josef Kozani might be more likely to grant an interview to journalists than to a student."

He ignored Frank's grimace. After all, getting to know someone from Petronia could turn out to be a help to them. Besides, they had kept up cover stories a lot trickier than this one.

This case could turn out to be a lot more fun than I thought, Joe mused.

"My brother is a total nut bar," Frank muttered to himself ten minutes later. He shoved his hands in his pockets as he looked for a second pay phone to use. They had strict orders to check in with the Gray Man every day. And since Joe was busy with Sofia, Frank had to make the call.

Frank could hardly believe Joe had offered to help Sofia get an interview with Josef Kozani. The two of them were off now, calling the major hotels in Athens to track Kozani down.

That was something he and Joe should be doing on their own, Frank thought. He didn't like the way things were starting out. Involving someone else could seriously jeopardize their case.

"One look at a pretty girl, and Joe's common sense takes a hike—to another planet," Frank said under his breath.

Even if Sofia was pretty, there was something about her that rubbed Frank the wrong way. Was it just a coincidence that she'd practically rammed them at the very moment they were about to follow Kozani into that taverna? Frank didn't see how she could know about their case, but he didn't trust her wide-eyed schoolgirl act, either. And she *was* from Petronia, the country that might be making a secret deal with Terry Brodsky for stolen Phoenix missiles.

Frank let his breath out in a rush. Being a Petronian citizen doesn't make her a criminal, he reminded himself. Still, every time he replayed their near miss with her moped, he came up with the same conclusion—Sofia could have stopped or steered clear of them if she'd wanted to.

So why hadn't she?

Glancing up ahead, Frank saw that the street he was on opened onto a square lined with trendy boutiques, galleries, and cafés. Shoppers and tourists, out in full force, were enjoying the hot weather. Frank spotted a kiosk about halfway down the block to his right. For the moment, it was empty except for the middle-aged man who ran it.

"Kalimera," the man said when Frank stepped up to the kiosk.

It sounded like a pretty standard greeting, so Frank said, "Hi. I'd like to make an international phone call, please."

The man smiled broadly and gestured to the phone that rested on the far edge of the counter. "You pay after," he said.

Frank nodded and dialed the number in Washington, D.C., that the Gray Man had given him and Joe. Keeping his voice low, Frank told the Gray Man about spotting Josef Kozani. "We're trying to track him down to the local hotels now," he finished.

"Good work," the Gray Man told him. "If Kozani's in town, there's a good chance that he's setting up the deal between Petronia and Brodsky. Be sure to stay on him. Anything else?"

Frank hesitated before answering. "There's a girl from Petronia, Sofia Alcalay . . ." He quickly told the Gray Man about their crash encounter with Sofia and her interest in Josef Kozani. "It couldn't have been a coincidence. But I didn't see anything on her in the background file. . . ."

"Let me punch the name into the data base here," the Gray Man told him. After a short silence, he said, "She looks clean. We have nothing on her."

Frank breathed a sigh of relief. "Great. I'll

keep my eyes open anyway." A couple came up to the kiosk just then, so he shifted the phone and said, "'Bye, Uncle Steve. I'll call again soon."

After he paid for the call, Frank stepped away from the kiosk. Might as well head back to the hostel and wait for Joe, he thought. He unfolded his map and traced the route he had taken from the taverna where they'd lost Josef Kozani. The student hostel where he and Joe were staying was a long hike across Athens, on one of the winding streets that climbed up the slopes of the Acropolis. So far, he and Joe had been using taxis to get around, but Frank decided he'd walk back. That way, he could get a better feel for the city.

Frank refolded the map and slid it back into his pocket. He was just putting on his sunglasses, when a familiar girl's voice called out to him.

"Frank Hardy! What are you doing in Athens?"

Frank turned toward the café he was passing, and his mouth dropped open. "Nancy?"

Nancy Drew was sitting at one of the café's square tables. A tennis visor held her reddish blond hair off her face, but it didn't hide the wide grin she shot him. She wasn't alone, either. Bess Marvin stopped talking to a guy at the next table and stared at Frank in surprise.

"Hey! What a great surprise!" Bess cried.

Both girls were wearing shorts and tank tops. They jumped to their feet as Frank jogged over to give them hugs. "Joe's not going to believe it when I tell him you two are here," Frank said, grinning from ear to ear.

"Where is he, anyway?" Bess wanted to know.

Frank shot a wary glance at the dark-haired guy next to Bess. "He's sightseeing," he said vaguely. It wasn't a total lie. Joe was probably spending a lot of time taking in the sight of Sofia Alcalay. Changing the subject, he asked Bess and Nancy, "So what brings you two to Athens?"

He was wondering if they were on a case. It was a reasonable guess, after all. Nancy had solved mysteries all over the globe and had teamed up with him and Joe more than a few times in the past.

Nancy seemed to know what he was thinking. "This is strictly a pleasure trip," she told him. "We're heading out to the islands in a few days, but we wanted to do some sightseeing in Athens first."

"Looks like you've been hitting the stores more than the tourist sights," Frank teased, nodding to the pile of bags that filled the third chair at the girls' table.

"I couldn't help it," Bess said, her blue eyes twinkling. "I mean, I *had* to get some of those cool leather sandals. Not to mention something for George, since she's at tennis camp and couldn't come with us. And you should see the jewelry!" She smiled sheepishly as she set the bags down on the ground so Frank could sit down. "I figure the Acropolis will always be there, but the good stuff in the stores could be gone in no time."

"Well, let me know when the credit cards run dry and you're ready to visit the Acropolis," the guy Bess had been talking to spoke up from the next table. "I'd like to see it myself."

Taking a closer look at him, Frank saw that he was in his twenties, tall, with a muscular build, curly dark hair, and smiling brown eyes set in a round face. He was checking out Bess with definite interest. Judging by the flush in her cheeks, something was brewing between them.

"Oh—Theo Papandreou, meet Frank Hardy," Bess said. "Frank and his brother, Joe, are good friends of ours."

Theo held out his hand to Frank. "Good to meet you," he said easily. "Don't let the name fool you. I'm Greek-American, and have spent my whole life in California. This is my first visit to Greece, believe it or not. My aunt and uncle live here in the Big Olive."

"The Big Olive?" Frank shot Theo a cockeyed glance. "You're kidding, right?"

Theo shook his head. "Sounds corny, but that's what my aunt and uncle call Athens—"

He broke off as a loud crash sounded from nearby, followed by loud, angry shouting in Greek.

Frank turned and his whole body went taut. He relaxed when he realized that it was just a couple arguing at a table behind them. One of them had thrown a glass, which had smashed on the sidewalk. The man was leaning forward in his chair, waving his hands furiously.

"Whoa. . . . This guy's serious," Theo whispered under his breath.

"What are they saying?" Nancy asked worriedly.

Theo took another look at the couple. "He's pretty angry. Saying something about how she'd better not go through with it."

"With what?" Bess asked, her eyes widening.

Frank tried not to pay much attention. It wasn't their business, after all. But the couple was so loud that it was hard to ignore them. The woman was wearing a hat and sunglasses—all Frank could see was her auburn hair twisted into a knot at the back of her neck. She said something in a low voice, and the man let loose with a scathing stream of words.

"Uh-oh," Theo said, glancing nervously at Nancy, Bess, and Frank. "I don't like the sound of this."

"What? What did he say?" Bess asked, alarmed.

Theo took a deep breath before answering. "That guy just threatened to kill her."

Chapter

Three

Nᴀɴᴄʏ ᴊᴇʀᴋᴇᴅ ʜᴇʀ ʜᴇᴀᴅ around to peer at the couple again. The color had drained from the woman's face, and she was clutching her glass so tightly her knuckles were white. The dark-haired man's angular face was so red that it looked as if he might explode.

"Should we do something?" she whispered to Frank, Bess, and Theo. "What if he's serious?"

She started to get up, then stopped when a waiter appeared with a broom. He said something to the couple in a low voice before bending to clean up the broken glass. Nancy was relieved to see the man lean back in his chair. He wasn't acting calm, but at least he had stopped shouting. The woman was obviously still flustered as she said something to the man, then hurried from the café.

When Nancy turned back to the man, he was

gesturing angrily at the woman's back. Then he threw some money on the table and stormed off.

"I hope they're going to be okay," Bess said, following the woman with her eyes.

"Me, too." Nancy tried to shake off the uneasy feeling that had come over her while she listened to the fight. "Anyway, it's over now, and we're here on vacation." She shot Frank a sly glance. "Right?"

He'd seemed distracted when she first spotted him—a lot more serious than if he and Joe were vacationing. She was pretty sure they were on a case, and the warning look Frank gave her told her she was right.

"Are you and your brother going to the Greek islands, too?" Theo asked Frank.

"We don't really have a plan," Frank said. "Joe and I figured we'd leave things open. You know, make up the trip as we go along."

You mean, as your case unfolds, Nancy thought. She was dying to find out the real reason the Hardys were there, but she knew secrecy could be vital to them. "Maybe we can all have dinner tonight," she suggested. "I'd hate to miss out on seeing Joe."

"Why don't you join us, too?" Bess asked Theo, but he shook his head.

"My aunt and uncle are making a special dinner for me tonight," he said. "I have to—"

"Hey!" Bess interrupted, pointing to the table where the arguing couple had been sitting. "That woman dropped her wallet."

A black leather wallet lay on the pavement under the chair where the woman had been sitting, and Bess jumped up to retrieve it. Flipping open the leather wallet, Bess pulled out a few cards. Nancy spotted a picture of the auburn-haired woman on one of them. "There's just one problem," Bess said, grimacing. "It's all in Greek."

"Here. Let me take a look," Theo offered. "My parents speak Greek at home, and they taught me to read it, so I'm pretty fluent." He took the cards from Bess. "Wow!" he said, shaking his head. "This belongs to Alexis Constantine."

"The daughter of that famous shipping guy?" Bess's mouth dropped open in surprise. "I can't believe we were sitting next to one of the richest women in the world!"

"I saw a show about her family on 'The World's Wealthiest People,'" Frank said. "Apparently, the Constantines' empire is huge. Shipping, trucking, airlines . . . you name it."

"Not to mention their own private island and a yacht that's probably bigger than my neighborhood back in River Heights," Bess added dreamily.

"Is there someplace where we can contact Alexis in Athens?" Nancy asked.

Theo inspected the cards, then shook his head. "The address on these is Kiros. That's the island the Constantines own near Crete."

"I don't think there's anything else important," Bess said. She slid her fingers into the wallet's folds, pulling out a folded card. "Just this postcard," she said. As she unfolded the card, a tattered paper napkin fluttered into her lap.

Nancy picked it up and looked at it. The napkin was edged with a Greek key design. "Taverna Garitsa, Corfu," Nancy said, reading the blue letters at the center of the napkin. "It must be someplace where European tourists go, since the name is printed in the Roman alphabet as well as in Greek."

Theo took the postcard from Bess. As he flipped it over to look at the printed inscription, Nancy caught sight of a picture of a sun-bleached, white church high on a hill overlooking the sea. "This postcard's from Corfu, too," Theo said.

"There's nothing written on it, though," Bess said. "I wonder why she'd keep these old things?"

It *was* curious, Nancy thought, handing the napkin back to Bess. "How are we going to locate Alexis here in Athens?"

"Constantine Shipping must have an office here," Frank put in. "Or at Piraeus. That's the major port, just west of here, on the Mediterranean."

"Let's also leave our telephone number with the owner of the café. That way, if Alexis comes back for her wallet, she'll know where to reach us."

"Here we are at the Andromeda Palace," Joe told Sofia later that afternoon. "According to the receptionist, this is where Josef Kozani is staying."

A taxi had just dropped them off in front of the seaside resort. Directly in front of them was a wide pink stucco building with a sign that read Registration and Reception in both Greek and English. Behind it, pink, yellow, and white stucco cottages were clustered among pine trees and lush, colorful gardens. The land sloped down toward the azure sea.

Earlier he and Sofia had spent over an hour calling hotels in Athens. They'd finally learned that Josef Kozani was registered at the Andromeda Palace, located on a wooded peninsula about six miles south of central Athens. Using his cover as a reporter, Joe had managed to get a villa for himself and Frank, too. He figured that they'd have an easier time keeping tabs on Kozani if they were all staying at the same place. Sofia had been so eager to find the man that they'd decided to head to the resort right away. Joe would go back to their hostel later to fill Frank in and pack up.

"Do you think Mr. Kozani is here now?" Sofia asked, biting her lip.

"I hope so," Joe answered. "But since I booked a villa for Frank and me, we're bound to run into him soon, even if we don't find him right away."

It took Joe only a few minutes to get his key and a map of the resort from the concierge. "Great news," he said when he rejoined Sofia outside. "I found out that Josef Kozani is staying in Villa Number Thirty-five. Frank and I are in Number Forty-one. They're probably not very far apart."

Sofia's dark eyes lit up. "How do we get there?"

Checking his map, Joe saw that one path led toward the villas from the registration area. A second path wound down the hillside to the resort's private beach before curving back up to the villas. Private beach, huh? Joe thought. He shot Sofia a sideways glance, then started down the path that led toward the beach. As long as they were here, it couldn't hurt to take a quick detour. . . .

The sun was low in the sky now. By the time they reached the deserted beach, the aqua water of the Aegean had deepened to navy. Ribbons of orange and red snaked across the cloudless sky.

"Pretty great, isn't it?" he asked.

Sofia nodded, her eyes shining. She turned away from the sea to stare up at him. "Thank you for letting me come with you."

Joe couldn't help smiling to himself. Here he was, with a pretty girl in a totally romantic spot. . . . He knew they should be getting to Kozani's bungalow, but he couldn't make himself move.

"It's too bad that Frank and I won't be here very long," he said. "I'd really like to—"

He broke off as a flash of light in the woods to the left of the beach caught his eye. He blinked and stared more closely. Something was definitely moving there.

Or someone.

Joe's sleuthing instincts went into overdrive. Maybe it wasn't anything suspicious, but he couldn't afford to ignore it. Not when a traitor to the United States *and* a dozen high-tech nuclear missiles could be involved.

Shooting a glance at his map of the Andromeda Palace, he saw that the area where the light had come from was at the tip of the peninsula that housed the resort. There weren't any paths or pools or gardens there. Just woods. Why would anyone be there?

"Joe?" Sofia's voice cut into his thoughts. "Is everything all right?"

"Sure," he said distractedly. "I mean . . . uh, no! Sofia, I really think you should go ahead to my villa."

"But why?" she asked, confused.

Joe frantically searched his mind for an explanation that wouldn't blow his cover. "I think I heard some kind of wild animal over there."

"Wild animal?" Sofia took a step closer to Joe and grabbed his arm. "Shouldn't we both leave?"

Joe shook his head, giving her the map and the key to his villa. "I'd better check it out and alert security," he said. "I'll meet you at my villa."

To his relief, she nodded. With a single backward glance at the surrounding woods, Sofia hurried toward the path that rose up the hillside to the villas.

As soon as she was gone, Joe ran to the woods. He moved quickly and quietly through the thick cover of pine trees, keeping close to the water. After he'd gone about a hundred yards, he stopped, unzipped his belt pack, and pulled out his binoculars.

It was hard to see clearly in the deepening twilight. Joe thought he saw some branches move and quickly focused in on them with the binoculars. But if someone was there, he or she was well hidden. "Come on," he urged under his breath, sweeping the binoculars slowly over the area. "Show me who you are."

Then he saw it again. Another flash of light. Joe zeroed in on the spot with his binoculars, then grinned to himself. "Gotcha!" he whispered.

The trucks were pretty well covered with branches, but there was no mistaking the long, boxlike shape or the glint of light off the cab's front grill. It looked as if there were two of them. And judging by the way the trucks were camouflaged, Joe knew they weren't there for an everyday delivery to the resort.

So what *are* you here for? he wondered. And what were those flashes of light? Some kind of signal?

He swept the binoculars out to sea. Lights sparkled from the boats heading to and from the port town of Piraeus, to the west. Most of the boats went past the Andromeda Palace far out to sea. But Joe noticed one barge moving slowly closer to the wooded coast—straight toward the spot where the two trucks were hidden.

The cargo on the barge was covered, but Joe quickly gauged its size. It seemed just about the same size as a half-dozen Phoenix missiles.

On deck was a squat, barrel-chested man. Joe couldn't see his face clearly, but there was a long, dark mark on his arm. Maybe a tattoo?

Moving as quietly as he could, Joe crept closer to the spot where the trucks were. He was still a couple of hundred feet from them, but by the time the barge got to the coast, he'd be in a perfect position to see. He hadn't caught sight of Terry Brodsky, but every instinct in his body told him that the Phoenix missiles were on that barge.

You've got the magic touch, no doubt about it, Joe congratulated himself. We've been here less than a day, and you've almost cracked this case wide op—

Ka-blam!

A deafening explosion rocked the entire wooded peninsula, sending Joe diving for cover. He threw one arm over his head and quickly grabbed his binoculars with the other. He put them to his eyes. This time he didn't have any trouble locating the spot. Huge flames rose up from the trucks' metal cabs, licking at the branches of the nearby trees.

The trucks had blown up!

Chapter

Four

JOE JUMPED TO HIS FEET. After shoving his binoculars back in his belt pack, he hurtled through the woods toward the burning trucks. If there were any people near those trucks, they could have been hurt!

Pine branches slapped at his face as he crashed through the woods. No need to keep quiet anymore, he thought. Everyone in the resort must have heard that explosion.

When he reached the small clearing where the trucks were, the light from the fire was blinding. Joe had to shade his eyes with his hand to look around. Searing hot flames billowed out of the cab windows, and a cloud of acrid black smoke stung Joe's lungs. After pulling the bottom of his T-shirt up, he used it to cover his mouth.

"Is anyone here?" he yelled. "Anyone need help?"

No answer. If anyone had been with the trucks, they must have taken off. *If* they'd been able to get out alive . . .

"Whoa!" Joe jumped as a flaming pine branch landed just in front of him. He stamped it out, then had to back away from the heat. The flames were shooting twenty feet into the air now. Sweat poured down Joe's brow. People would be arriving any minute to put out the fire. If he was going to take a look around, he'd better act fast!

He quickly made a circle around the two trucks, looking both at the ground and the trees nearby. He was searching for tracks or bits of clothing that might have caught on branches—anything to tell him who might have been here and why.

But if someone had been there, he had been very careful. There wasn't a single clue.

A prickly feeling on the back of Joe's neck made him whirl around. All his instincts told him that someone was out in the woods, watching him. But he saw nothing except pine trees blending into the murky darkness. Get a grip, Hardy, he thought, shaking himself.

The wail of a siren sounded in the evening air. Peering through the trees, Joe saw flashing red lights moving his way. Slipping into the woods, he started in a wide circle around the lights, heading back toward the private beach. He definitely did *not* want to answer any questions about what he was doing there.

By the time he emerged from the thick pine trees, many guests had gathered on the beach. Before joining them, Joe hung back at the edge of the trees and stared out at the water. He'd forgotten all about the barge. Now it was nowhere in sight.

Where had that barge gone? he wondered. If it had turned around and moved back out to sea, it must have gone quickly and suddenly—which supported his suspicion that the person he'd seen on board was up to no good. Ferrying the Phoenix missiles to the two trucks in the woods?

It made sense. If the explosion hadn't happened, and if the barge were carrying the stolen missiles, the missiles could have been transferred to the trucks and then driven to Petronia, or whatever their final destination was. Joe didn't think any missiles could have been destroyed along with the trucks. If they had, the explosion would have been bigger. A lot bigger.

Joe took a deep breath and let it out slowly. There sure were a lot of ifs and unanswered questions. Such as, who had blown up the trucks? And why? He glanced back at the flames, which were slowly being brought under control by firefighters. Apparently, he and Frank weren't the only ones trying to stop Brodsky from trucking the missiles to Petronia. But who else even knew—

"Joe!"

Joe looked over to find Sofia running toward him on the beach, her face tight with worry. "I came down when I heard the terrible noise. What happened?"

"Some kind of explosion, I guess," he hedged. He avoided her gaze. "I'm not sure, exactly." His eyes fell on the slender silhouette of a man a few yards behind Sofia. Even in the semidarkness Joe had no trouble recognizing his carefully trimmed beard and mustache. "Hey, it looks like Josef Kozani is curious about the fire, too."

"Great!" she crowed. "Let's go talk to him."

"We don't want him to feel like we're badgering him," Joe put in. "Maybe I should talk to him alone first. Once I butter him up, he'll probably be happy to talk to you, too." What he really wanted was a chance to find out what, if anything, Kozani knew about the missiles *and* this explosion. And he couldn't do that with Sofia around.

"Well—all right," she agreed with a frown.

Joe jogged over to the businessman. "Excuse me . . . Mr. Kozani?" he asked.

At first Kozani didn't appear to see him. His expression was tense, his eyes glued to the fire.

"I'm Joe Hardy, a reporter with *Business World Weekly,*" Joe said, citing a popular magazine.

Finally Kozani turned toward him. "Reporter? I do not recognize your name." His eyes were suspicious as they flickered over Joe. Then he gave an impatient wave and added, "Never mind. Do you know what has happened here?"

"Explosion," Joe answered. "Now, if we—"

"An explosion of what?" Kozani interrupted. As he took a few more steps toward the woods, Joe noticed a blood vessel pop out on his forehead. And he nervously worked his fingers together. He seemed a lot more interested in the fire than any idle bystander should be. Maybe he *was* involved in setting up a deal to buy the missiles for Petronia. If someone was trying to wreck the deal, it would explain why Kozani was so upset.

"Mr. Kozani, I'd like to talk to you about—"

"If you want an interview, you must call my press secretary and make an appointment, like everyone else," the businessman cut him off. He started to walk away, but Joe grabbed his arm.

"Wait! I, uh, thought you might make an exception. You see, I'm here with a student from—"

"A student?" Kozani scoffed. "Please, do not waste my time any longer." Shaking off Joe's hand, he strode toward a handful of firefighters who were resting at the edge of the woods. One of the men began talking seriously to Kozani. When Joe walked up to them, another firefighter stopped him. The man didn't speak English, but his gestures were very clear. Obviously, this area was off limits.

"Unless you're an internationally famous businessman, like Josef Kozani," Joe murmured.

He let out a sigh. He wasn't going to get any information out of Kozani for the moment. Joe walked slowly back to Sofia, who was waiting at the edge of the beach. "Kozani won't talk to us tonight. He's too busy," he told her, without going into detail. Seeing her disappointed expression, he added brightly, "I'm sure Frank and I will be talking to him within the next few days, though. When we do, we'll put in a good word for you."

"Well—thank you for trying." Sofia sighed, and her eyes flickered to where Josef Kozani was still talking to the firefighters. "In that case, I guess I will go back to my student apartment."

"How about having dinner?" Joe blurted out. Then he remembered all that he and Frank still had to do—check out of their hostel and move their things to the Andromeda Palace. Plus, they had to find out what Josef Kozani was up to. "Tomorrow night," he added.

Sofia smiled, brushing her long dark hair over her shoulders. "I would like that," she said.

"Great," Joe replied with a grin. "Okay. Let's get a taxi back to the main part of Athens. I'll drop you off."

"Our first night in Athens, and we're already rubbing elbows with the rich and famous," Nancy said a few hours later. She, Bess, Frank, and Joe were squeezed into a small taxi that wound up a cobbled street just below the Acropolis. Stores and restaurants lined the narrow lane on both sides. "This is what I call a vacation!"

"I'll say," Bess agreed. "Alexis could have just sent a chauffeur or someone to pick up the wallet. It was really nice of her to invite us to hear Greek music with her and her father."

"All of us," Frank added. "Thanks for picking us up at our hostel. It saves us from finding a taxi to lug our stuff." He tapped the duffel bags wedged beneath their feet in the back of the taxi. "This way we can head right to the Andromeda Palace when we leave the club later."

Alexis had contacted Nancy and Bess at their hotel that afternoon, after returning to the café to look for her wallet. Alexis and her father already had plans to spend the evening at a *rebetiko* club, so she suggested that Nancy and Bess meet them there. After hearing that the girls already had plans with friends, Alexis insisted that the whole group come along.

"I'm still in shock," Joe said, turning in the front seat to grin at Nancy and Bess. "I can't believe you're in Athens, too. It's really great to see a couple of friendly faces."

Nancy gave Joe a sympathetic smile and reached forward to ruffle his wavy blond hair. Frank had filled her in on the details of their case when he called to tell her and Bess that they were moving. She knew how frustrating it was to have a case go haywire.

"I'm glad you guys could take a break to come with us tonight," she said. "From what I hear, *rebetiko* is really great. Kind of like a Greek version of urban blues."

"This is the place," Bess announced, looking out the window.

The taxi had stopped in front of a stuccoed building with a sign out front that read Taverna Dionysos. Even through the closed door, Nancy could hear singing and the rich strumming of instruments. After paying their taxi driver, the group hurried into the club.

Inside, the first thing Nancy noticed were the musicians. Half a dozen men played guitarlike instruments in a song that sounded like traditional Greek music with a rich, bluesy feeling. In front of the musicians, half a dozen men danced in a circle. Tables were crowded around the edge of the dance area, with men and women eating, talking, or clapping along to the music.

"Excuse me. Are you Nancy and Bess?" a woman next to Nancy asked.

Nancy recognized Alexis Constantine immediately. Now that she wasn't wearing sunglasses, Nancy saw that her eyes were an interesting shade of pale green. Her auburn hair was pulled back in a sleek knot at her neck. She wore a gold necklace and an expensive-looking, sleeveless white dress that showed off her tanned skin. Nancy also noticed dark circles under Alexis's eyes.

Nancy introduced herself, Bess, and the Hardys and then reached into her shoulder bag and pulled out the leather wallet she'd found at the café.

"Thank you very much for bringing this back," Alexis told her and Bess. "There are things in here that I could not bear to lose." Opening the wallet, she eagerly pulled out the tattered napkin and postcard from Corfu. "Thank goodness they're still here," she murmured.

"We're glad we could help out," Bess said, smiling. She pointed at Alexis's necklace—a gold chain whose links repeated an intricate geometric design. "That's absolutely gorgeous."

"It is a Greek key design," Alexis explained. "It belonged to my mother."

"Alexis!" A tall man with a deep, booming voice came up and clapped an arm around Alexis's shoulders. He appeared to be in his forties, with jovial dark eyes and a round stomach that pressed against his shirt. He'd obviously been dancing. His thick dark hair was a little wild, his shirt wrinkled and untucked, and his forehead moist with perspiration.

"Papa, these are the people who found my wallet," she said. "Nancy, Bess, and . . ." She looked blankly at the Hardys.

"Frank and Joe Hardy," Frank supplied. "We're journalists. Nice to meet you, Mr. Constantine."

"You must call me Christos," Alexis's father insisted. He gazed at his daughter with such warmth and spirit that Nancy couldn't help liking him. "How can I thank you for making my Alexis smile again?" He beamed at them. "I would be happy for Alexis to make some new friends. You must join us tomorrow for a cruise on the *Island Princess.*"

Bess's eyes lit up. "Your yacht?" she asked.

Alexis nodded distractedly. "Papa, I'm sure they must have other plans. . . ."

"Thanks for the invite, but Frank and I won't be able to make it," Joe put in. "Business, you know."

"Then you two must come," Mr. Constantine said to Nancy and Bess. "I will not take no for an answer," he warned. "You have been so kind, you must allow me to give you my personal thanks."

"If you put it that way . . ." Bess said after glancing at Nancy and receiving a nod.

"It is settled, then," Mr. Constantine said. "Is that not wonderful, Alexis?"

"Yes, of course," Alexis said flatly. She gave Nancy and Bess a lukewarm smile, then waved for a waiter. "Our guests must be hungry, Papa."

Within seconds Nancy, Bess, and the Hardys were sitting at a table right next to the musicians.

After making sure that they were settled, Alexis and her father sat at the next table, where a few other people were talking and eating.

"What was bothering her?" Frank asked in a low voice, flicking a thumb at Alexis.

"She didn't exactly seem excited about the idea of having us as her guests again tomorrow, did she?" Bess whispered.

Nancy shrugged. "Maybe she's still upset about the fight she had with that guy," she said. "Wow!" she added as two waiters appeared with trays of shrimp, stuffed grape leaves, spiced rice, and lamb kebabs. "This looks delicious."

For the next half hour Nancy forgot about Alexis and enjoyed the food and music. The musicians had to take a break eventually, and Nancy, along with everyone else in the club, stood to give them a standing ovation. One of the musicians, a wiry older man with steel-gray hair and glasses, walked past their table holding an instrument that looked like a cross between a guitar and a mandolin.

"You guys were awesome," Frank told him, leaning back in his chair to grin at the man. "What's that instrument? I don't think I've ever seen one."

The man nodded his thanks. "This is a bouzouki," he said, holding it out. "I have been playing it for years, since Christos Constantine was just a boy."

"You know the Constantines?" Bess asked, leaning forward over the table.

As if in answer, Mr. Constantine came over and greeted the older man warmly. "Bravo, Yannis! I see you have met Alexis's new friends."

"We are just getting acquainted," Yannis told him.

While Mr. Constantine went over to talk to some people at a table across the club, Yannis gestured to the waiter to bring him something to drink. Then he moved over to an empty chair between Nancy and Joe and sat down. "I am Yannis Apollonious," he told them. "My nephew, Elias, was Christos's closest boyhood friend. Later they were business partners."

He smiled around the table while the teens introduced themselves and explained how they had met Alexis. "Is your nephew here tonight?" Bess asked, glancing around.

Yannis shook his head sadly, letting out a sigh. "Elias passed away, many years ago."

"I'm sorry," Nancy said simply, unsure what else to say.

Finally Joe leaned forward and said, "I didn't know Mr. Constantine had a partner."

Yannis took a drink from the glass the waiter brought him. "Yes," he said. "I watched Christos and Elias build the shipping company together. Those were wonderful days, before Elias became sick. . . ."

Yannis didn't mind talking about such a personal subject. "Unfortunately, my nephew's bad health forced him to sell his half of the business to Christos," the old man continued. "It is a great sadness that he could not live to see what a success Christos has made of the company."

"That's for sure. Mr. Constantine is the envy of people all over the world," Frank put in.

Yannis nodded, then held up a warning finger. "But it is a great responsibility, too. Worrying about his daughter . . . Christos's wife died when Alexis was just a baby, you know. My grandnephew, Petros, is a great help to him, though. He is Christos's right hand, as you say."

Again Nancy was struck by how personal Yannis was getting. But it *was* an interesting story. "You must be very proud of your grandnephew," Nancy said, smiling at Yannis.

The old man's eyes sparkled in his wrinkled face. "Yes, I am proud. Petros was given nothing. He worked his own way up in the company. He was engaged to Alexis until a few days ago."

"What happened?" Bess wanted to know.

Yannis gave a shrug. "Alexis broke it off, just like that," he said, snapping his fingers. "All she would say is that it wouldn't work out. Christos was as disappointed as Petros, perhaps even more so. He had been hoping to unify the two families." He shook his head sadly, taking a drink from his glass. "It has been a hard week for Christos," he went on. "First, Calliope Dalaras, his biggest rival here in Greece, attempted a hostile takeover of Christos's airline, Aegean Air. And then, the trouble with Alexis and Petros . . .''

"Wow," Nancy said, shooting Alexis's father a glance over her shoulder. "And here he is, acting as if he doesn't have a care in the—"

"Is there room for one more?" Nancy turned to see Theo Papandreou standing behind her, grinning at them.

"Theo!" Bess exclaimed, her whole face lighting up. "I thought you were with your aunt and uncle."

Theo squeezed around the table and sat at the last empty chair, next to Bess. "I was. But when I explained that there was a girl I absolutely had to see or I would die of a broken heart, I guess they didn't want to have that on their consciences."

"How did you find us?" Nancy wanted to know.

"I called Bess earlier and asked where you were going—just in case," Theo answered, never taking his eyes from Bess's flushed face.

Yannis got to his feet and nodded around the table. "We will talk again," he said amiably. "Now I must eat before we begin playing again."

As Yannis went over to Alexis's table, Bess leaned close to Theo and said, "That guy's known the Constantines forever. He just gave us their whole life story."

"Greeks are like that," Theo said, chuckling.

"For them it's normal to talk about personal stuff even with people they hardly know. But look out . . ." Theo raised a teasing eyebrow. "Next thing you know, he'll be grilling you about *your* secrets."

As he and Bess talked, Nancy let her eyes roam idly around the club. Mr. Constantine was still chatting with a couple across the room. Alexis was smiling and listening to Yannis, but she seemed detached. Nancy couldn't stifle the feeling that something was preoccupying her.

As Nancy watched, Yannis said something to Alexis, then got up and went over to speak to one of the other musicians on the platform. Alexis sat back and reached into her bag. Surprise showed on her face, and a second later she pulled a folded sheet of paper out. When she looked at it, her face went completely white.

Immediately, Alexis crumpled the paper in her hand. She jumped to her feet, her eyes darting frantically left and right.

What's going on? Nancy wondered. Why was Alexis suddenly so scared? Getting to her feet, Nancy started toward Alexis. "Alexis, are you—"

Before Nancy could finish the question, Alexis slung the strap of her purse over her shoulder and ran from the *rebetiko* club.

Chapter

Five

WORRY WASHED OVER NANCY as she stared after Alexis. Something was very wrong. People in the club were so busy eating and talking that they hadn't even noticed that Alexis was upset.

"What's up, Nancy?" Frank asked, leaning toward her. "Why did Alexis leave like that?"

Glancing over her shoulder, Nancy saw that Bess and Theo were still talking, their heads bent closely together. "I'm not sure, but she acted really upset," she said. "I'm going after her."

"Count us in," Joe said, getting up from the table and moving toward the exit.

Outside, Nancy spotted Alexis hurrying up the narrow street toward the Acropolis. As she walked, Alexis was turning her head frantically, as if she expected to see someone. She seemed so desperate that Nancy's heart went out to her.

"Alexis!" Nancy called. "What's the matter?"

Alexis peeked back over her shoulder, then gasped when she saw Nancy, Frank, and Joe. Without answering, she started running up the steep street.

"What was *that* all about?" Joe muttered as he, Nancy, and Frank took off after her.

"We want to help!" Frank called. But a second later Alexis disappeared around a sharp turn.

When Nancy, Frank, and Joe rounded the turn, Nancy could see that they were gaining on Alexis. Her dark shadow was just fifty yards ahead of them now. Up above, the Parthenon's marble columns were lit with yellow spotlights that cast an eerie glow into the night sky.

Nancy willed her body to move faster, but it wasn't easy in a skirt and floppy sandals. By the time they finally caught up to Alexis, she was just outside the entrance to the Acropolis.

"Alexis . . . stop!" Nancy said breathlessly.

As she, Frank, and Joe drew even with her, Alexis finally gave up. She came to a halt, her chest heaving. Wisps of her auburn hair had come loose, and her eyes were wet with tears.

"I needed to . . . get some fresh air," she gasped. "That is all."

Nancy caught the doubtful glance Frank and Joe shot each other. "We don't mean to bother you," Frank assured Alexis. "We just wanted to make sure you're all right."

"I am fine," Alexis said, but she was still glancing around and acting skittish.

Seeing the crumpled-up paper in Alexis's hand, Nancy said, "I don't mean to pry, but was there something in that note that upset you?"

The fear in Alexis's eyes intensified for the briefest moment. Then she seemed to shake herself. "It is nothing." She waved the paper, as if to prove her words.

Nancy decided to let it drop. She'd spotted a few Greek symbols on the paper, but she didn't see any way to find out whàt they meant. Besides, whatever was bothering Alexis was her own business. She just hoped Alexis wasn't in any danger. . . .

When Nancy, Joe, Frank, and Alexis walked back into the Taverna Dionysos a few minutes later, Nancy was happy that the musicians had started to play again.

"There you are!" Bess called out. She jumped up and came over to them, with Theo behind her. "What happened? Why'd you pull that sudden disappearing act?"

"Sorry," Nancy said. She could see that Alexis was still nervous, so she decided to play down what had happened. "We, uh, just needed to get some air."

Alexis held herself stiffly. "I must get back—"

She broke off as the door to the club opened and a man walked in. Nancy did a double take when she saw him. It was the man Alexis had been arguing with that afternoon! He was short, with a compact build and angular features. He glanced briefly at Alexis, then frowned when she turned away from him without a word and walked back to her table.

"What's *he* doing here?" Frank asked Nancy in a low voice.

Before Nancy could answer, she heard Mr. Constantine's booming voice call out, "Petros!" He stepped past Nancy and began talking to the man.

"Petros, huh?" Joe echoed, giving him a sideways glance. "He must be Yannis's grandnephew, Mr. Constantine's second in command. Why are you guys acting as if he was on last week's episode of 'America's Worst Criminals'?"

"Because he threatened to kill Alexis this afternoon," Bess answered in a whisper.

"I bet Petros was pretty steamed when Alexis called off the wedding," Nancy said. "Maybe that's what they were fighting about—"

She was interrupted by an outburst from Alexis's father. He and Petros were speaking in Greek, but Mr. Constantine's angry gestures told Nancy that he wasn't happy.

She studied the younger man's angry expression. Petros had threatened Alexis once today, at the café. Could it be that he had slipped some kind of threatening note into her bag then, too?

Nancy quickly shook away the thought. It's none of your business, she told herself firmly.

Alexis herself had said that the note wasn't anything. Still, Nancy couldn't shake the niggling suspicion that more was going on than Alexis had said.

Frank glanced uneasily at Christos Constantine and the young man who'd just arrived. For the last five minutes the two men had been speaking together urgently.

"Hey, you guys," Frank said, leaning close to his brother, Nancy, Bess, and Theo. "It looks like they're dealing with some pretty heavy stuff. Maybe we should think about leaving."

Nancy, Bess, and Joe all nodded their agreement.

"Good idea. They probably don't want to worry about entertaining us if there's some kind of problem," Nancy said. "I'll tell Alexis good night for all of us."

"Okay. We'll wait outside," Bess said. She tapped Theo's arm, but he was listening so intently to Mr. Constantine and Petros that he didn't seem to have heard her. "Theo?" she repeated.

"Huh?" Theo finally tore his gaze away from the two men. "Sorry, did you say something?"

Bess laughed, tapping him on the forehead. "Anyone home in there? We're going. Come on."

Frank was about to follow them, when Mr. Constantine stepped over to him and Joe, bringing Petros with him. "My good friends," Alexis's father said, gazing back and forth between Frank and Joe. "You two are reporters, are you not?"

"That's right," Joe answered.

Mr. Constantine clapped Petros around the shoulder and said, "This is Petros Apollonious. He handles many of the business interests for my companies. Trucking, shipping, airlines . . ."

"Nice to meet you," Frank said, holding out his hand to Petros. He introduced himself and Joe, then asked, "Is there something special you needed?"

Mr. Constantine answered. "We have just had some very bad news," he said, drawing his bushy brows together in a frown. "Someone blew up two of our trucks at the Andromeda Palace, on the outskirts of Athens."

Frank shot his brother a meaningful glance. So those trucks were owned by Constantine Shipping! That might just add a new angle to the case, if Joe's theory that the trucks were waiting to transport missiles was true. If Constantine Shipping was involved, then this was a golden opportunity to find out more about what had happened.

"Wow. That's a tough break," Joe said. "Do you have any idea who did it?"

Petros shook his head no, but Mr. Constantine declared, "It was Calliope Dalaras. I know it!"

That name definitely rings a bell, Frank thought. Hadn't that bouzouki player mentioned her? "She's your competitor, right?" he asked Mr. Constantine.

Petros nodded. "Calliope just tried to buy Aegean Air from Mr. Constantine. She did not succeed, but—"

"And this is how she gets revenge," Mr. Constantine broke in angrily. "I won't stand for it."

"Uh, what exactly do you want Frank and me to do, Mr. Constantine?" Joe asked. Frank could see how impatient his brother was to find out more about the missiles. "Perhaps we could write an article, you know, exposing Calliope Dalaras. . . ."

"That is precisely what I was thinking," the older man said.

"We'll need background information," Frank put in quickly. "Where the trucks were going, what was on them—that kind of thing."

Constantine didn't bat an eye. "Of course," he said. "Whatever it takes to make sure that Calliope does not get away with this."

"We should not do anything we might regret," Petros said, shooting an uneasy glance at his boss. "Shouldn't we consult with the police before—"

"The police will be told," Christos interrupted. "But I will also take this matter into my own hands." He turned to Petros and said firmly, "Set up an interview for tomorrow morning."

Frank could hardly keep himself from letting out a victory yell. Talk about a lucky break! But all he said out loud was, "Sounds good. Any time."

"I'll say one thing for Kozani," Frank said the next morning as he and Joe stepped out of their villa. "He has good taste. This place isn't bad."

"If we run into him—and I hope we don't— we'll have to tell him how much we appreciate investigating him in such cushy surroundings," Joe said sarcastically. He closed the door behind them, then led the way down the path toward the beach.

After waking up, Joe had called the resort's operator twice and asked to be connected to Josef Kozani's villa. Both times there had been no answer. Since the businessman apparently wasn't in, Joe and Frank decided to sneak into his villa to see if they could find anything connecting him to Terry Brodsky or the stolen Phoenix missiles.

Villa 35 was set into the hillside just above the private beach. Joe cast an appraising eye over the pink stucco exterior and perfectly trimmed flowering bushes, then headed for the door.

"Hello?" he called, knocking on the door. He assumed the place was empty, but it didn't hurt to play it safe.

"Come on," Frank urged from right behind him. "Let's get in before someone sees us."

Joe tried turning the knob, but the door was locked. "Piece of cake," he mumbled. Unzipping his belt pack, he took out his lock-pick set and went to work. Seconds later he heard a click, and the door swung open noiselessly.

"Thank you, thank you. No need for applause," Joe said. He started to take a bow, then stumbled as Frank pushed him inside the cottage.

"Come on, Houdini. We've got work to do, remember?" Frank said, rolling his eyes. He locked the door behind them and took a few steps inside.

Joe was already taking in the details of the villa. Carpeted living room with a window overlooking the sea, kitchen area . . . "Looks like the bedroom's back there," he said, pointing to a hallway leading to the rear of the villa. "I'll check it out."

He was already in the hallway when Frank called softly, "Hey! Isn't that a briefcase?"

Sticking his head back into the living room, Joe watched as his brother pulled a leather briefcase from under the couch. "I don't know why he'd bother keeping it out of sight down there," Frank said. "Unless he's got something to hide."

"Like the fact that he's setting up a deal for Petronia to get the Phoenix missiles from Terry Brodsky?" Joe guessed. He was next to Frank in a flash. "Come on, open it."

Frank hit the buttons on the case, but the lid stayed shut. "It's locked—"

He broke off and whipped his head toward the door. "It's Kozani! He's back!" he whispered.

Joe heard the doorknob rattling and the metallic jangling of keys. "Oh, no!" he mouthed.

While Frank slid the briefcase back under the couch, Joe checked out the room. Before he could figure out where to hide, a key scraped in the lock.

Kozani was about to catch them red-handed!

Chapter

Six

WE'VE GOT TO HIDE!" Frank whispered. "And fast!"

There wasn't time to get to the back room. Frank made a running dive for the kitchen area off the living room. Joe tumbled in behind him just as the door to the bungalow clicked open.

Frank heard footsteps on the carpeting, then flinched when he saw a hand reach for the phone attached to the wall above the kitchen counter. It was Kozani, just a few feet away!

Judging by the expression in Joe's eyes, Frank knew what he was thinking: If Kozani headed into the kitchen—maybe three small steps from where he was—he'd find them, and their whole case would be ruined.

Frank hardly let himself breathe. On the other side of the counter, Kozani spoke into the phone in what Frank figured to be Greek or Petronian.

Kozani talked for just a minute or two and hung up. Frank heard the soft padding of feet on the carpet, then the click of Kozani's briefcase. After a few moments the door to the villa opened and closed again. A key was turned in the lock.

Getting to his knees, Joe peered over the top of the counter. "He's gone. Come on, Frank. This time, we're not going to lose him."

"I'm with you on that one, brother." Frank jumped to his feet and ran to the small window next to the door. "He's heading up the path to the reception area," he said.

Frank unlocked and opened the door, and he and Joe slipped outside. They kept a safe distance behind Kozani as the businessman headed for a taxi at the resort's main entrance. As soon as he got in, Frank and Joe sprinted for the next cab.

"We're in a hurry!" Joe told the driver. "Follow that taxi!"

Frank quickly realized that Kozani was heading toward the center of Athens. After about twenty minutes, Kozani's car pulled over to the curb about half a dozen car lengths ahead of them.

"He's stopping," Frank said, recognizing the huge, teeming square they were in. "Syntagma Square. We'll get out here," he told their driver.

Joe pulled some bills from his wallet and handed them over. *"Hasta la vista,"* he said, hopping out onto the sidewalk.

"That's Spanish, Joe," Frank said with a groan. But his eyes were still focused on the slender, well-dressed figure of the businessman ahead of them. "Come on, before we lose him."

He and Joe loped after Kozani, skirting shoppers and sightseers. At the far side of Syntagma Square, Kozani crossed a street and headed straight for a crowded café. He paused outside, glancing uncertainly at the groups seated at the outdoor tables.

"Hold up," Joe said, stopping before he and Frank crossed the street. "Looks like he's meeting someone, doesn't it?"

Up ahead, Frank saw Kozani walk purposefully among the tables until he stopped at one in particular. Frank glanced quickly at the person who was sitting there, then did a double take.

"That's Sofia!" Joe said in a low voice. "What's *she* doing here?"

Frank heard the surprise in his brother's voice, but he was too busy observing to answer. At the table, Sofia Alcalay smiled up at Josef Kozani and shook his hand. Then Kozani sat down and the two started talking intently. "I *knew* there was something suspicious about her," Frank muttered.

When he turned to his brother, he saw that Joe was frowning. "Don't jump to conclusions," Joe said. "Maybe she managed to get an interview for her thesis on her own. We're supposed to have dinner tonight. I'm sure she'll tell me about it then."

"Maybe," Frank said doubtfully. "But didn't you say that Kozani wouldn't give you the time of day? That he didn't have time for students?"

Joe didn't say anything. "I mean, how do we even know she's a student?" Frank went on.

"There's one way to find out," Joe said. He fished in his pocket for some change. "You stay here. I'm going to call Athens University."

When Joe came back a few minutes later, the expression on his face was very grim.

"She's not a student?" Frank asked.

Joe shook his head. "There's no Sofia Alcalay registered," he said. He looked across the intersection to where Sofia was still talking with Josef Kozani. "I don't get it. Why would she lie to us?"

"I don't know what her game is," Frank said. "All we know is that she may be from Petronia, which desperately wants to build up its arms arsenal. And here she is, meeting a guy who could be trafficking in illegal arms. This at the time when some Phoenix missiles might be for sale on the black market."

Joe let out a resigned sigh, glancing at his watch. "Oops. It's almost noon, and our meeting at Constantine Shipping is at twelve-thirty."

"The Gray Man said to keep tabs on Kozani," Frank said, nodding back at the café. "You go ahead and meet with Petros. I'll keep an eye on these two."

"Am I dreaming, or is this one of the most perfect spots in the entire world?" Bess Marvin grinned and sat up in her lounge chair on the deck of the *Island Princess*, the Constantines' yacht.

"It's beautiful, all right." Nancy looked out at the azure waters, glinting with sunlight.

All morning she and Bess had been the guests of Christos and Alexis Constantine. The girls had met the Constantines in the vast Constantine Shipping complex at the port town of Piraeus, where the *Island Princess* was docked. Ever since leaving the dock, the yacht had been winding among the islands of the Saronic Gulf, outside Athens. Now Nancy saw that they were headed toward an island whose hills were studded with stucco houses, olive trees, and chalky cliffs. "Ever since we left the dock behind this morning, I've felt as if we've been sailing through a picture-perfect postcard," she said dreamily.

"Not to mention that you and your dad have been totally spoiling us," Bess added, turning to Alexis.

That was an understatement, Nancy thought. The day had started with a tour of the *Island Princess*. The yacht had everything—a Jacuzzi, sumptuous living and dining areas, and staterooms filled with intricately carved teak woodwork. Once they had set off from the dock, Alexis's father had provided a steady stream of information on the area, and the ship's cook had supplied iced tea and delectable snacks. Minutes earlier, Mr. Constantine had gone to ask the cook to bring them their lunch.

"Thanks for inviting us to spend the day with you, Alexis," Nancy added. "It's a real treat to get an insider's tour of the area."

Alexis sat up in her lounge chair and fingered the gold necklace around her neck. "It is the least we can do to repay you for returning my wallet," she said, giving Nancy and Bess a weak smile.

Alexis had been perfectly cordial, but there was still something reserved and standoffish about her. Nancy felt that Alexis would be far happier if she and Bess weren't around.

"Here is lunch," Mr. Constantine said in his booming voice.

Nancy turned to see him stepping out on deck from the yacht's steering house. He was wearing swim trunks and an unbuttoned short-sleeve shirt that revealed his tanned torso. A uniformed waiter followed him with a tray of food, which he placed on a table near the lounge chairs. Nancy's mouth started watering when she saw a platter of small red fish wrapped in some kind of leaves. Two other platters held spiced rice with vegetables, and a salad with olives, capers, and the most luscious-looking tomatoes she had ever seen.

"Please, you must try the *barbounia se klima-tofila,*" Mr. Constantine said. "Red mullet in grape leaves."

The yacht had just been anchored in a crescent-shaped cove surrounded by smooth, low rocks. Lush hills covered with olive trees and wildflowers, rose up behind the rocks. Nancy could hear a speedboat buzzing somewhere nearby, but there wasn't a single person in sight.

"This is Spetses," Mr. Constantine said as the plates of food were being prepared for everyone. "Centuries ago the people from this island were known as master sailors and shipbuilders. Now Spetses is a place where many prosperous Athenians have vacation homes."

"I can see why," Nancy said. "It's gorgeous."

She and Bess dug into their food with gusto, but Alexis didn't touch anything on her plate. She pushed it aside, then got to her feet and stood looking out over the railing at the cove. "I'm really not hungry," she said. "Perhaps I will go for a swim while you eat. Would you mind?"

"No, of course not," Nancy said. Alexis's father looked as if he were going to object, but before he could, Alexis took off the blousy white tunic she wore over her bathing suit and dove into the crystal water. As she swam toward the rocks with sure strokes, her father stared after her.

"I am sorry for my daughter's behavior," he said, frowning. "Alexis has been so moody lately,

I do not understand her. I thought it would be good for her to make some new friends."

Nancy didn't want to pry into the Constantines' private lives, but she didn't want to seem unsympathetic, either. "If she's going through a hard time, maybe she just doesn't feel like putting on a happy face for people she doesn't know."

"You are intelligent," Mr. Constantine said, a slow smile spreading across his face. "I have learned to judge people. It is one of the things that has made me a success. But still I do not understand why my own daughter broke off her engagement." His eyes were filled with worry, and Nancy couldn't help feeling sorry for him.

"To Petros Apollonious, right?" Bess said. In answer to Mr. Constantine's surprised expression, she quickly added, "The bouzouki player last night mentioned it."

Alexis's father nodded, letting out a sigh. "Yannis. Of course."

Nancy shifted her gaze to the cove, where Alexis was just pulling herself onto one of the rocks. As she stretched out on its sunny, smooth surface, a movement at the water's edge caught Nancy's eye.

"Looks like we're not the only ones here," Bess said, nodding toward the cove.

A scuba diver's head had just broken the water's surface about a dozen feet from the rock where Alexis was.

"This island is full of grottos and coves," Mr. Constantine said. "Divers come looking for sponges and corals—" He stopped speaking as a loud, terrified scream sounded from the rocks. "Alexis!" he cried.

Nancy whipped her head back toward the rocks in time to see the scuba diver grab Alexis by the arm. A wet suit and mask covered him from head to toe. Nancy could tell that it was a man and that he had a tall, powerful build, but that was all.

"Hey! Let her go!" Bess cried, but the scuba diver paid no attention. Wrapping one arm around Alexis's throat, he started to pull her over the rocks.

"Stop him!" cried Mr. Constantine. "That man is trying to kidnap my daughter!"

Chapter

Seven

Nancy jumped up from her lounge chair and ran for the yacht's railing. In one quick motion she leaped onto it and made a flying dive into the water. Her head broke through the surface seconds later, and she could see Alexis and the scuba diver struggling on the rocks. Alexis was trying to resist, but the man was much bigger than she was.

"Stop!" Nancy yelled. Two splashes behind her told her that Bess and Mr. Constantine were in the water, too, but she didn't have time to look. "We have to cut him off!" she yelled.

She took off through the water with a powerful crawl, heading toward the rocky point at the end of the cove. The scuba diver was just reaching the rocky ledge at the tip of the cove. In a minute he'd disappear on the other side with Alexis!

Hearing Alexis's cries for help, Nancy urged

herself to go faster. Seconds later she was pulling herself onto the rocks at the edge of the cove. Alexis and the scuba diver were just a few yards ahead of her, climbing to the top of the rocky ledge. Breathless and dripping with seawater, Nancy scrambled up after them.

"I am here," Christos Constantine said from behind her.

For half a second the scuba diver paused to glance over his shoulder at them. Taking advantage of his hesitation, Nancy lashed out with a judo kick to the man's chest. The kick threw him off balance, sending him over the top of the rocky ledge. The attacker tried to pull Alexis with him, but Mr. Constantine flew forward from behind Nancy and grabbed his daughter's arm.

"Papa!" Alexis cried with relief as he pulled her from the scuba diver's grasp.

Now that Nancy was at the top of the ledge, she saw that a speedboat was moored on the other side of the rocks, just out of sight of the cove. Alexis's attacker had quickly regained his footing and raced nimbly down to the floating craft. In a flash the speedboat was in the open gulf.

Alexis was sitting on a nearby rock. "Are you all right?" Nancy asked.

Alexis nodded. "He did not harm me," she said, but her face was pale and her voice tight with fear.

"We must contact the police immediately," her father said.

"No!" Alexis cried, grabbing his arm.

After what had just happened, Nancy would have expected that Alexis would *want* to contact the police. "That person could have kidnapped you—or worse," she said.

"We must arrange for you to have a bodyguard around the clock," Mr. Constantine said firmly to his daughter. "You must have protection."

"Papa, *please,*" Alexis begged. "I cannot bear to have guards following me. It is like having two shadows. I do not think that I am in grave danger."

Not in danger? Nancy thought. Why was Alexis playing down the seriousness of what had happened? "Do you have any idea who that man was, Alexis?" she asked. "Or why anyone would want to hurt you?"

Alexis shook her head. Thinking back to the night before, Nancy said, "You don't think this had anything to do with the paper you found in your bag at the *rebetiko* club last night?"

"Paper? What paper?" Mr. Constantine asked.

"It was nothing," Alexis said quickly. "Papa, you must believe me. I do not think it is necessary to worry the authorities over nothing."

Her father frowned out at the water for a long moment. Then he snapped his fingers, turning back to his daughter. "If you do not want a bodyguard, perhaps Nancy and Bess will do us the kindness of being our guests here on the *Island Princess*," he suggested. "That way, you would not be alone. . . .'"

"Papa," Alexis said, her green eyes flitting nervously back and forth between Nancy and Bess. "I really do not think they want to—"

"We're only going to be in Athens a day or two longer. Maybe we shouldn't interfere," Bess added, not wanting to get between Alexis and her father.

"It is as you wish," Mr. Constantine said. "But in that case, I must insist upon a guard, Alexis." She opened her mouth to object, but he cut her off. "I will not leave you open to more attacks."

Alexis closed her mouth and sagged back against the rock. After a moment she glanced moodily at Nancy and Bess. "We can have staterooms prepared as soon as we return to Piraeus," she said flatly. "Will you stay?"

Nancy didn't want to accept the invitation if Alexis didn't want them there. On the other hand, if keeping Alexis company would lessen the chances of her being attacked again . . .

"Sure," Nancy told Alexis. "Bess and I can check out of our hotel later today."

Frank took a drink of his soda, then peeked over the top of his newspaper at Sofia Alcalay and Josef Kozani. Over two hours had passed since he and Joe had followed Kozani to this café. Soon after Joe had left for his appointment at Constantine Shipping, a waiter had served lunch to Kozani and Sofia. Frank knew then that they'd be there for a while, so he'd slipped across the street and sat at a table on the opposite side of the café. So here he was, wearing sunglasses and hiding behind a newspaper someone had left behind.

He was just thinking about ordering a second lamb kebab sandwich, when Kozani signaled the waiter for their check. Seconds later he and Sofia got up and shook hands. Sofia headed off down the sidewalk, while Kozani went to the curb and waved for a taxi.

"Looks like it's show time," Frank said under his breath. He threw some money on the table, then started after Josef Kozani. Frank didn't trust Sofia, but following Kozani was his number one priority.

Up ahead, the Petronian businessman was just getting into a taxi. Frank ran to the curb, but there wasn't an empty taxi in sight. Kozani's car was already disappearing around a corner.

"This can't be happening," Frank groaned.

Stifling his frustration, he quickly retraced his steps to the café. If he could only catch sight of Sofia, the stakeout wouldn't be a total bust. . . .

Yes! Frank spotted her blue dress about half a block ahead of him. She was walking at a pretty fast clip, as if she was in a hurry to get somewhere. Frank's eyes narrowed as he jogged a little closer. He didn't know what she was up to, but he was definitely going to find out.

A few minutes later Sofia went into a store. It was a travel agency, judging by the posters in the window. Frank waited a few stores away, pretending to window-shop. When Sofia came back out again, she continued down the street. Frank started to follow again, then stopped in front of the travel agency. What had she been up to in there? he wondered.

On a whim, he pulled the door open and went inside. He found himself in a small office with framed travel posters along the walls. The office held two desks that were piled high with papers, calendars, and tickets. Only one desk was occupied, by a robust middle-aged woman wearing a red suit and lots of makeup. She said something to Frank in Greek. When he stared blankly at her, she switched smoothly to English.

"Can I help you?" she asked.

"I was supposed to meet my fiancée here," Frank fibbed, pretending to look around for someone. "She's pretty, with dark hair, about this tall." He put his hand up to his shoulder.

The woman gave Frank an apologetic smile. "I am afraid she already left," she told him. She reached for some papers on her desk, acting concerned. "She did not mention anything about a second ticket."

"I'm not surprised," Frank said, making up his

story as he went along. "She was going to travel while I took care of business here in Athens. I just found out a few minutes ago that I may be able to go along with her after all. Could you tell me the exact time she'll be leaving?"

When the travel agent hesitated, Frank said urgently, *"Please.* I'd like to surprise her."

The woman took a deep breath, then gave him a conspiratorial smile. "Yes, of course," she agreed. "And the Greek islands are so romantic."

"So I've heard," Frank told the woman, breathing a sigh of relief. He sat in one of the chairs in front of her desk while she slid a copy of a ticket over to him. Luckily, it was printed in English as well as Greek. It was a ferry ticket from Piraeus to the island of Crete, leaving that same evening.

Crete, eh? Why was Sofia going *there?* She hadn't mentioned anything to him or Joe about a vacation. Frank stared at the ticket, trying to reason it out. Crete was the farthest south of all the Greek islands, but Petronia was to the north of Greece. If Sofia were involved in an illegal scheme to purchase the Phoenix missiles for Petronia, why go to Crete? It didn't make sense.

"Shall I write up a second ticket?" The travel agent's voice broke into Frank's thoughts.

He blinked and looked over at her. "Oh . . .

Thanks, but maybe I'd better wait until I, uh, get the final okay from my boss." Frank made a mental note of the city where the ferry would dock: Chania. "Did she make a hotel reservation?" he asked.

"No, but I could suggest some excellent hotels. . . ."

"No, thanks," Frank said. "We may be staying with friends."

Back out in the hot sunshine, he was still wondering about Sofia's plans. Going to Crete didn't make sense if she was mixed up in a plan to buy Phoenix missiles. Maybe Joe was right and she wasn't involved. But then, why feed them that phony story about being a student at Athens University? And if she wasn't doing a thesis on Josef Kozani, then why was she talking with him in that café just now?

Frank let out his breath in a rush. So far, he and Joe had a lot of questions. He just hoped they started coming up with some answers. . . .

"Would you like some more coffee, Mr. Hardy?" the receptionist at Constantine Shipping asked Joe.

"No, thanks," Joe answered, tapping his foot impatiently against the marble tiles of the reception area. It had been over an hour and a half since he arrived to meet with Petros Apollonious about the "article" he and Frank were supposed to be writing on Calliope Dalaras and the trucks that had been blown up. But so far, all he'd seen was the reception area.

He'd already drunk three cups of coffee and checked out every square inch of some cool-looking ceramics that were displayed—plates, pitchers, and vases that had scenes from ancient Greece painted on them. The receptionist had buzzed Petros twice, but both times Petros said he would be with Joe "soon." Joe was beginning to think that would be sometime in the next century.

"Mr. Hardy?" Joe looked up to see Petros standing there in a navy suit with brass buttons. "I'm sorry to keep you waiting," Petros said, raking a hand through his short dark hair. "The police called with more questions about last night's explosion."

"No problem." Joe jumped to his feet and went over to Petros, shaking the man's hand. "Have they found out who blew up the trucks?"

"They could tell me nothing," Petros answered grimly. "Come. We'll talk in my office."

He led the way down a hallway to a large office overlooking the docks. Petros's sleek desk stood in front of a floor-to-ceiling bookcase. Next to the windows were two black leather chairs and a matching leather sofa. Petros took a seat on the sofa and gestured for Joe to take a chair.

"Frankly, I do not think there is much for you to write an article about," Petros began.

"Christos thinks that Calliope Dalaras is responsible, but we have no clues to back up his assumption."

"Well, why don't you and I see what we can come up with on our own?" Joe suggested. He flipped open the notebook that he'd bought just before going to the shipping company. "We can start with the basics. Like, can you tell me what was in those trucks and where they were going?"

"I just went over this information with the police," Petros said wearily. He got to his feet and went over to his desk, then hesitated. "That is odd. The record book was on my desk earlier. . . ."

Joe glanced quickly around the office, then pointed to a ledger on the table next to the open windows. "Is that it?" he asked.

"Yes, of course." Petros walked quickly over to the table and reached for the ledger. Then he froze, his eyes fixed on something outside.

Joe stood up and followed Petros's gaze. He saw that a yacht had docked in front of the shipping office. Alexis Constantine was just stepping onto the dock, wearing a white tunic that billowed in the breeze. She was followed by her father, Nancy, and Bess. "Back from their cruise already, eh?" Joe commented.

"Yes," Petros said.

While Joe and Petros watched, Alexis said something hurriedly to the rest of the group, then walked quickly away. Instead of heading toward the entrance to the Constantine Shipping offices, she hurried toward a huge building that looked like some kind of garage. Through a wide-open doorway, Joe could see a few truck cabs. He didn't miss the way Petros's gaze stayed glued to Alexis until she disappeared inside the building. Apparently, he still had feelings for her.

But that's not why you're here, Joe reminded himself. "Um, about those trucks?" he prompted.

Petros blinked and looked at him in surprise. Joe had the feeling that Petros had forgotten he was even there. "Yes. Of course," Petros said. He picked up the record book and came back to the couch. He was just setting it on the table in front of Joe when the phone on his desk rang.

Joe tried to stifle his impatience while Petros strode over and answered the phone. He spoke in Greek for a few minutes before hanging up. When he turned back to Joe, he appeared worried. "I am afraid you must excuse me for a few moments," he told Joe. "Our business is so large and diverse. I am afraid there are always problems to take care of. I will be back . . ."

"As soon as you can," Joe finished. He flashed Petros a resigned smile. "Take your time, Petros."

Petros disappeared through the doorway, leaving Joe alone. Just what I need, he thought. Another interruption. But, hey, as long as I'm waiting . . .

Leaning forward, Joe flipped open the cover of the record book Petros had just placed on the table. He *was* about to show it to me anyway, Joe thought. I doubt he'll mind if—

Suddenly a loud crash sounded from somewhere outside Petros's office. Joe jumped to his feet, frowning.

He was already halfway to the door when he heard an ear-splitting scream that chilled him.

Chapter

Eight

"Dɪᴅ ʏᴏᴜ ᴛᴡᴏ ʜᴇᴀʀ ᴛʜᴀᴛ?" Nancy paused outside the chrome-and-glass entrance to Constantine Shipping. "It sounded like someone screaming."

"Oh, no," Bess said. "Do you think something happened to—"

She didn't have to finish her sentence. After the attack at the cove, Nancy knew they were all thinking about Alexis. Mr. Constantine's jaw tightened and a muscle twitched above his jawbone. He moved quickly to the door and flung it open, mumbling something to himself in Greek. Nancy and Bess were right behind him as he ran inside.

Nancy's eyes flew around the sleek reception area, but she didn't see Alexis. A ceramic plate was smashed on the marble floor. Next to the broken shards stood a short, sturdy woman in

her forties, wearing an expensive-looking skirt
and jacket. She had wide-set dark eyes in a round
face, and her short black hair was perfectly
styled. There was something elegant about her,
but she also had the determined stance of an
angry bulldog.

"Calliope!" Mr. Constantine burst out, facing
off with the woman. He said something to her in
Greek, and the two immediately began shouting.

"Hey, there's Joe," Bess whispered, nudging
Nancy with her elbow.

A circle of men and women had crowded into
the reception area. Nancy guessed that they'd
come from all over the company after hearing
the scream. Joe was standing with them at the
end of a carpeted hallway that led deeper into the
building.

"He's probably here for that interview he and
Frank told us about last night, when we all left
the *rebetiko* club," she told Bess. "I don't see
Petros, but he must be around here somewhere."

Joe gave them a little wave. Nancy thought
he'd come over to them, but instead he started to
back away slowly from the reception area and
move down the hallway. Apparently, he was
going to take advantage of the chaos to do some
snooping. Crossing her fingers, Nancy silently
wished Joe good luck.

Joe stepped quietly into Petros's office and
shut the door behind him. As long as everyone

was busy getting an earful of the screaming match of the century, he might as well look at the record book.

"And learn what I can about those trucks," he mumbled aloud.

Going back over to the leather chair, Joe opened the book—and let out a groan. It was filled with columns of neatly written information, but it was all in Greek.

"Just my luck," Joe muttered, shaking his head.

Just then the door to Petros's door swung open. Joe straightened up with a gasp as the receptionist stepped in, carrying a pile of folders.

"Uh, hi!" Joe said brightly, stepping quickly away from the record book. Inwardly, he breathed a sigh of relief. The receptionist didn't seem to have noticed that he'd been snooping.

"I was wondering," he added, shooting the young woman a wide smile. "Petros had to step away for a minute, but I'm in kind of a hurry. Would you mind translating some of these entries for me?" Seeing her hesitate, he quickly added, "Mr. Constantine wanted me to write an article about the trucks that were blown up. Please. It's very important."

For a moment Joe thought she was going to refuse. Then she came over to him, smiling shyly. "I did hear Mr. Constantine mention a reporter," she said slowly. "My English is not very good, but I will help as much as I am able. . . ."

"I'm sure you'll do fine," Joe assured her, grinning. "I need to know everything you have on the two trucks. Their cargo, where they were going . . ."

She placed the pile of folders on the table, then stared at the book, running her finger down the entries. She stopped at two entries near the bottom of the page that had already been circled with a red pen and read the small print. "First is the name of the client who hired the trucks. . . ."

"So Constantine Shipping leases out trucks to other companies?" Joe asked.

"Yes," she answered with a nod. "In this case, the client was K and B Imports."

Joe didn't remember seeing that name in any of the background material the Gray Man had given them. "Okay," he said, jotting it down in his notebook. "What was in the trucks, and where were they going?"

"Let me see . . . The materials on the trucks were electronics from Japan. They arrived in Piraeus yesterday on one of our cargo ships," she explained. "And the destination was"—she slid her finger across to the next column in the entry—"an address in Athens."

"Would you mind writing it down?" Joe asked. He opened his notebook, handing it to her. While she wrote down the information, Joe glanced at the record book. There was one more column for each of the trucks, he saw. He pointed to it and asked the receptionist, "What does that say?"

"It is the name of the driver," she explained. "Luckily, the drivers of those two trucks were not inside when they exploded."

Joe thought for a moment. If the drivers hadn't been in the trucks, where *had* they been?

"Tell me something. Do the clients provide their own drivers?" he asked.

"Oh, no. All drivers are employed by Constantine Shipping," the receptionist answered.

Joe grinned. At least he didn't have to travel far to track them down. "Do me a favor," he said. "Write down their names, too, all right?"

Chances were, the drivers knew more about the explosion than anyone else. One way or another, Joe thought, he was going to find a way to talk to them.

For the last ten minutes, Nancy and Bess had been pretending to blend into the decor while Calliope Dalaras and Christos Constantine yelled at each other. Nancy couldn't understand their words, but the tone made it clear that this wasn't a friendly chat.

Finally, Calliope threw up her hands. With a final angry exclamation, she turned on her heel and stormed back outside.

The door had barely closed behind her when it opened again. Nancy half expected that Calliope Dalaras was coming back for a final shot, but instead Petros appeared. He said something to Mr. Constantine in Greek. Nancy heard him mention Calliope's name. The two men spoke briefly, and then Petros started down the carpeted hallway toward his office.

"Petros!" Nancy called urgently. She didn't know what Joe was up to, but whatever it was, she didn't want Petros to catch him.

Petros stopped and turned to face Nancy, giving her and Bess a quick nod. "Yes?" he asked.

"I was, uh, just hoping that you and Mr. Constantine could tell us what that fight was all about," Nancy said.

"Yes!" Bess added quickly. "What was that woman so angry about?"

Petros came back into the reception area, but it was Mr. Constantine who answered. "Calliope Dalaras has the nerve to pretend that she did not destroy my two trucks," he said, growing angry all over again. "Just because the police chose to question her about the trucks, she accused *me* of trying to ruin *her* with rumors."

"Wow. I wonder why?" Nancy said. Out of the corner of her eye she spotted Joe coming down the hallway toward them. A young woman was with him. She slipped behind Christos Constantine and Petros and sat at the reception desk. Joe tapped a pad he held and gave Nancy a subtle thumbs-up sign. Then he stepped smoothly over to her, Bess, Petros, and Mr. Constantine.

"What's going on?" he asked. "I heard a lot of screaming out here."

Before anyone could answer, the receptionist interrupted. "Mr. Constantine?" she said. "There is a telephone call for you. Will you take it in your office?"

"No," he answered. "I will take it here." He strode over to the desk and grabbed the phone, barking into it in Greek.

As he listened to the person on the line, Nancy saw his face tighten. His fingers gripped the receiver so tightly that his knuckles turned white. "What is it?" she asked.

He covered the mouthpiece before answering. "It's Alexis," he said, his voice a hoarse whisper. "She's been kidnapped!"

Chapter
Nine

KIDNAPPED?" Nancy tried to control the feeling of dread that welled up inside her.

"But . . . how?" Bess asked. "I mean, Alexis was with us until about fifteen minutes ago—"

"Shhh!" Petros interrupted. He nodded to the reception desk, where Mr. Constantine still held the telephone receiver. He was shaking, his face a sickly gray. As he barked a few Greek words into the receiver, his voice sounded distraught.

"Someone, get him a chair," Nancy said as the receptionist was already pulling hers out.

Mr. Constantine didn't even seem to know they were there. For a few moments he nodded, as if in answer to something the other person said. Then he hung up the phone and sank against the receptionist's chair.

"How could someone do these terrible things to my little Alexis?" he finally said in a voice that trembled with emotion. His whole body seemed to sag. "First she is attacked at Spetses. And now . . . this."

Nancy's heart went out to him, but she knew they had to focus on getting Alexis back. "What exactly did the kidnappers say?" she asked gently.

"That I must wait for further instructions," Mr. Constantine answered. "If I call the police or talk to anyone from the media, my daughter will die." He turned to Joe with flashing eyes. "You must not report this. Alexis's life depends on it."

"You have my word," Joe promised. "Did you recognize the voice? Was there anything special about it?" he asked. Nancy could practically see the gears turning in his head as Joe tried to see how the kidnapping might fit into the stolen missiles he and Frank were trying to track down.

Christos Constantine shook his head. "The voice was muffled. I could not even determine whether a man or a woman was speaking. But I know who is responsible," he said angrily. "It is Calliope. It must be! She is bitter because her attempt to buy Aegean Air was not successful. First she blew up my trucks, and now she is trying to destroy my family."

It sounded like a pretty extreme way of getting revenge, Nancy thought. "But Calliope was right here with all of us until seconds before the kidnappers called," she pointed out.

"Do you think she was trying to distract us?" Bess asked.

Petros's dark eyes flashed with excitement. "That is exactly right!" he burst out. "She must have arranged for someone else to kidnap Alexis while she was arguing with you, Christos."

"It's possible," Nancy said slowly. She eyed Petros carefully. He seemed awfully eager to implicate Calliope, but Nancy hadn't forgotten the angry threat that Petros himself had made to Alexis. "Petros, you were outside," she said, trying to sound casual. "Did you see anything suspicious?"

Petros's eyes narrowed for a brief second. Then he shook his head. "Nothing at all," he answered. "Perhaps the guards at the security gate saw something, though."

While Petros reached for the phone, Joe stepped up to Nancy and Bess. Leaning close to Nancy, he whispered, "Having second thoughts about Constantine's number two man?"

She nodded. Seeing that Mr. Constantine was hovering close to Petros, she said to Joe, "What was he doing outside when he was supposed to be interviewing you?"

"Good question," he said. "We were watching from his office when you guys got off the *Island Princess*. Right after Alexis took off, Petros got kind of distracted, like he had something on his mind. That was when he suddenly had to leave. Said he had to check on some problem."

Before Nancy could say anything else, Petros hung up the phone, and he and Mr. Constantine turned back to her, Bess, and Joe. "Security saw nothing unusual. Only two vehicles have passed through the gate in the past half hour," Petros told them. "Calliope Dalaras's car and one of our own trucks."

"Do you think Alexis was in one of them?" Bess asked worriedly.

"Could be," Nancy said. "One thing seems pretty definite, though. Alexis was with us when we got off the *Island Princess* just a half hour ago. Whoever the kidnapper is probably struck right here at Constantine Shipping. The person could have taken Alexis in Calliope's car or that truck, or—"

"She could still be here," Bess finished. "Why don't we start a search? Maybe we'll find some clue to who kidnapped her."

Petros shook his head doubtfully. "The grounds are vast. There are the docks, the office, warehouses, trucking facilities . . . It would take days to examine."

"Then that is what we must do!" exclaimed Mr. Constantine, slamming his palm onto the reception desk. "We are talking about my only daughter. We must do whatever is necessary to get her back safely."

"Petros and I saw her go into a big building after she left the yacht. Looked like a garage," Joe put in.

"Ah, yes," Mr. Constantine said, brightening. "There's a room in there where Alexis goes when she wants to be alone here in Piraeus. Let us go there right away."

"Go ahead," Petros said, holding back while the others headed for the chrome-and-glass door. "I'll stay behind and supervise a search of all the docks and buildings."

Nancy wasn't sure she trusted him, but he *was* Christos's most valued employee. Until she had something that specifically linked him to Alexis's kidnapping, she decided not to say anything.

A few minutes later Alexis's father led Nancy, Joe, and Bess into a large garage that was set back from the docks. The cavernous space was filled with trucks lined up in rows. There was a row of lockers along the wall to their left. Just beyond them, a doorway led to a room that looked like a lounge. Nancy could see a few men in coveralls sitting around a table that had coffee cups and plates of sandwiches on it. Two other men were getting into the cab of a truck that was near the huge, open doorway. Otherwise, the garage seemed quiet.

Mr. Constantine threaded between the trucks to a door at the rear of the garage. He pushed it open, revealing a small room. It held a comfortable couch and chair, and a desk with a portable stereo on it. There was a blue-and-white woven rug on the floor, and white lace curtains fluttered in the open window. The room seemed cozy compared to the storage shed.

"It's really kind of nice," Bess murmured, stepping inside.

"This room used to be an office," Mr. Constantine explained. "But Alexis has kept it as her own for years."

As Nancy entered the room, her gaze fell on something small and gold on the floor. "Hey!" she said, dropping to her knees. "Look at this!"

Christos Constantine, Joe, and Bess, all bent over her as she held up the tiny gold object. "Looks like a clasp."

"I bet it's from Alexis's necklace," Bess said. "So she must have been here!"

Mr. Constantine took the clasp from Nancy and stared at it with haunted eyes. "I cannot be sure, but . . . I think you are right. I am almost sure I remember her wearing the necklace on the yacht."

"Her kidnapper could have pulled it off when he took her," Joe said.

Nancy had been thinking the same thing. Taking a closer look around, she noticed that several CDs were scattered on the floor. There was a rip in the lace curtain, too, as if someone had yanked on it. "It looks like there was a scuffle, too," she commented, bending to pick up the CDs. "Apparently, Alexis didn't go quietly."

"Maybe one of the drivers saw something," Joe suggested.

"Perhaps," Mr. Constantine said as he led the way to the truckers' lounge.

While he spoke to the men, the others waited just outside the lounge. Nancy couldn't begin to imagine what Mr. Constantine was going through. For his sake, as well as for Alexis's, she hoped he found some clue to where Alexis had been taken. But when he rejoined them a few minutes later, he still looked grim.

"Did you find out anything?" Bess asked him.

"Only what we already learned from the security desk, that just one truck has left in the past hour or so," Mr. Constantine answered. "Georgious Roussos, one of our drivers, said that the cargo was a shipment of ancient Greek sculpture."

Nancy saw Joe take a peek at the pad he'd been holding. "Roussos, huh?" he murmured. He shot a quick look back into the lounge, then eyed the rows of lockers just outside the lounge door.

The name obviously meant something to Joe. Maybe the driver Mr. Constantine had mentioned tied into the stolen missiles or the trucks that had been blown up. Nancy was dying to find out the details, but she couldn't with Mr. Constantine around.

Seconds later Joe raised his eyebrows at Nancy and nodded silently toward the wall of lockers outside the truckers' lounge. She got the message—get Christos Constantine out of there so Joe could do some investigating on his own.

Turning to the older man, she steered him away from the lounge. "Maybe we should check the record book back in the office to be sure," she said.

"I'll catch up with you inside," Joe said, shooting Nancy a grateful smile. "I, uh, just want to get a soda in the lounge."

Luckily, Mr. Constantine was so distracted by his daughter's disappearance that he barely heard Joe. As he, Bess, and Nancy headed out of the garage, Nancy said, "Did the driver mention where the sculpture was being trucked to?"

"To the museum at Delphi," he answered. "It is due to arrive there this evening."

"Delphi?" Bess echoed. "That was one of the most important sanctuaries in ancient Greece, right?"

Alexis's father nodded distractedly. "That is right. Men would come from miles away to hear the oracle's prophecies," he said. "But I do not understand. Do you think the kidnappers would take my Alexis there?"

"It's only a guess," Nancy answered. "But it's definitely worth checking out. The truck that left from here was the only vehicle other than Calliope's to leave in the past hour. If she doesn't turn up here, I think that Bess and I should take a trip to Delphi. Apparently, the secret powers of the oracles aren't the only mystery there. . . ."

* * *

Early that evening Frank Hardy lay back in his lounge chair beside the pool at the Andromeda Palace. He'd been there all afternoon, ever since he'd followed Sofia Alcalay to the travel office in downtown Athens. Back at the resort, he'd been lucky enough to spot Josef Kozani going into his own villa. Kozani's bungalow was nestled into the hillside just above the pool. From his poolside chair, Frank had a perfect view of the man's door, without being too obvious. So far, Kozani hadn't moved from the place.

"This is the kind of case work I like," Frank mumbled to himself as Joe appeared.

"Yo, Frank," Joe called, jogging around the pool toward him. "I hate to interrupt your hard work."

Frank grinned up at his brother. "It's a tough job but someone's got to do it." More seriously, he asked, "Did you find out anything at Constantine Shipping?"

"A lot more than I bargained for," Joe said. "I talked to the driver of one of the trucks that was blown up, a guy named Roussos. He didn't speak much English, but I understood enough to get the basics of his story."

"And?" Frank prompted.

"Apparently, a couple of guys with guns forced him and the other driver from their trucks and hijacked them," Joe went on. "The hijackers were wearing masks. Roussos didn't seem to recognize Terry Brodsky's name, but he did say he saw a tattoo of a mermaid on the arm of one of the hijackers."

Frank let out a low whistle. "Didn't you say that the guy you spotted on the barge that night had a tattoo?" he asked.

"Correct," Joe answered. "I bet he and Brodsky parked the trucks in the woods before the guy with the tattoo went off and got on the barge with the missiles. That is, if the missiles were on that barge. We still don't know that for sure. Our only other lead is the company that hired the trucks in the first place." He flipped open his notebook and ran a finger down a page of notes. "K and B Imports. Their address is on some road called Iraklidon."

"It's almost seven. Any business is probably closed by now," Frank said, checking his watch. "We'll have to wait until morning to check it out." He got to his feet and looked up at Kozani's bungalow. "It's pretty quiet here. I say we make a very quick call to the Gray Man to let him know what's going on."

"Then you can head back here and keep an eye on our number one suspect," Joe said. "I have a dinner date I'm almost late for, so I can't join you."

It wasn't until they were outside their villa that Joe dropped another bombshell—that Alexis Constantine had been kidnapped.

"What!" Frank exclaimed. "How did that happen?"

Joe stuck his key in the door and pulled on the door to open it. "Someone got to her on the grounds of Constantine Shipping—" He broke off, giving the door a tug. "Hey, why's this thing so hard to open?"

As the door moved toward them, Frank was alerted by a metallic click that something was wrong. He glanced toward the kitchen area— then froze. A metal fishing spear was just being launched from a speargun on the counter. It was aimed straight at Joe's head!

Chapter

Ten

JOE SAW THE SPEAR whizzing toward him at lightning speed. *"Nooo!"* he cried.

His eyes squeezed shut as he instinctively dropped to the floor. All he could think was that he hadn't moved fast enough. He couldn't have, the spear was so close. A split second later the spear hit with a loud, wood-splintering crunch. Joe's entire body was still tensed as he waited to feel the searing pain of metal ripping into his flesh. . . .

"Joe! You all right?"

Joe cracked open one eye, then the other. He gingerly moved his arms and legs. He could hardly believe it, but everything still worked. "It didn't hit me." Still dazed, he sat up. Frank was crouched a few feet away, staring at him anxiously. "You're okay, too?" Joe asked.

Frank nodded. His jaw tightened as he got up

and tapped the spear, which was embedded in the bungalow's door. "Somebody wants us to back off this case—permanently," he said grimly.

"Which means we must be making progress," Joe said with a wry smile.

Looking over at the speargun, he saw that a wire had been attached to the trigger. The other end of the wire was nailed to the top of the door. "The door was booby-trapped," he realized. "When I pulled it open, the wire was yanked tight enough to release the gun's trigger."

"Serious stuff," Frank said, shaking his head. "The question is, who did it?"

"Kozani?" Joe guessed. "Maybe he knows we've been tailing him."

"Or, he could have warned Brodsky that we're on their trail," Frank went on. "Brodsky has the special forces training to set this up."

"I guess it could have been the guy with the tattoo, too," Joe said. "Though I don't know how he'd know we're in Athens, much less why."

When he looked at his brother, Frank was staring at him with an expression Joe couldn't quite read. "There's another suspect we have to consider, too," Frank told him. "I know you're not crazy about the idea, but—"

"Sofia didn't do it," Joe interrupted, guessing what his brother was getting at. "Okay, so maybe she's not being totally honest with us. But trying to *kill* us?" He shook his head adamantly.

Frank didn't say anything, but Joe could tell he wasn't convinced. "We have a date for dinner tonight," Joe went on.

"I hate to tell you this," Frank said, "but Sofia's leaving for Crete tonight."

"Crete?" Joe stared at Frank in disbelief.

Suddenly the telephone rang in their kitchen area. Joe hurried across the room and reached carefully around the speargun to grab the receiver. "Hello?"

"Joe? Is that you?"

Joe recognized the voice at once. "Hi, Sofia. We're still on for dinner tonight, right?"

"That is why I am calling," Sofia said. "I am sorry, but I must cancel."

"Cancel?" Joe echoed, frowning. "How come?"

"I did not realize how far behind I am in my studies," Sofia told him.

"Studying, huh?" Joe said. "It's too bad you can't do something a little more fun—like take a trip."

Sofia let out a little laugh. "You are teasing me. I cannot take any vacations until my thesis is finished," she said. Joe wasn't sure, but he thought she sounded just a little nervous. "Oh! I am sorry, but my roommate needs to use the phone. I will talk to you soon, Joe. Goodbye."

Before Joe could say anything else, the line went dead. He couldn't stop the suspicions that flooded his mind. Sofia had never mentioned a roommate before. . . .

"Bad news?" Frank asked.

"I'll say." Joe let out a sigh as he hung up the phone. "Let's just say that I'm starting to see what you mean about Sofia."

·

"What a day," Bess said as she and Nancy got out of a taxi in front of their hotel that Thursday evening.

"That's for sure," Nancy agreed. After spending the rest of the day with Mr. Constantine and a private detective, searching for Alexis, she was totally exhausted.

"I can't believe Mr. Constantine's security people or detectives haven't come up with any more leads," Bess said. "All we know is that two vehicles left the shipping compound . . . Calliope Dalaras's car and that truck that was delivering artifacts to Delphi."

"Maybe our trip to Delphi will turn up something the detectives he hired haven't found," Nancy said hopefully. "Mr. Constantine said that the drive takes a few hours. We'll have to make the trip tonight, so we can be at the museum there first thing in the morning."

Nancy led the way into the hotel lobby, which had terra-cotta tiled floors, dark beams, and white stucco walls with watercolors of Greek scenery hung on them. Potted plants and wooden benches were scattered about, giving Nancy the impression that she was in a small village inn. A stout man with gray hair stood behind the inn's reception desk. When he saw Nancy and Bess, he smiled and said, "*Kalispera*. Good evening, girls. There is a visitor here to see you." Leaning forward over the counter, he winked conspiratorially. "A handsome young man . . ."

He nodded toward a wooden bench.

"Theo!" Bess exclaimed. "I thought you were going to be busy tonight."

A grin spread across Theo's round face as he got up and moved toward them. "I talked them into letting me spend another evening with you."

"That's great," Bess said.

"There's just one problem," Nancy said, giving Bess a sympathetic glance. "We have to drive to Delphi this evening."

"We may be back sometime tomorrow, though," Bess was quick to add. "If we are, why don't we have dinner tomorrow night."

Theo grimaced. "I can't," he said. "My aunt and uncle are taking me on a tour of some of the islands. We're leaving tomorrow night." He fingered a small, ceramic amulet that hung from his neck on a silver chain.

"Hey, that's cool," Bess said, nodding at the amulet. "I like all those triangles and lines. They almost seem to make a picture."

"This? I picked it up at the market here in Athens," he said. He tucked it under his shirt, then ran a hand through his curly dark hair. "I don't suppose there's any way you could put off your trip for a day?"

Bess shook her head. "Alexis Constantine was kidnapped," she said before Nancy could stop her.

"This is very confidential information. You can't tell *anyone,*" Nancy told Theo. "Alexis's life could depend on it."

For the next few minutes Theo listened while Nancy and Bess told him about the attack at Spetses, the kidnapping, and their plans to track down the truck that had left Constantine Shipping for the museum at Delphi.

"Wow," Theo said when they were finished. He shook his head in amazement. "Could you use an extra person to help out in Delphi? I could come along."

"That'd be great!" Bess exclaimed before Nancy could protest.

Nancy hesitated to get any more people involved. After all, the kidnapper had threatened to kill Alexis if Mr. Constantine went public. But Bess was beaming at the prospect of spending more time with Theo, and Nancy couldn't bring herself to say no.

"Well," she said, smiling at Theo, "I guess we *could* use an extra pair of eyes and ears."

Frank paused in the evening twilight to look at his brother. After Joe was nearly killed by the speargun planted in their villa, he and Frank decided to act—fast. They were now on the path to Josef Kozani's seaside villa.

"Here's the deal," Frank said. "If Kozani planted that speargun, he's not going to be expecting to see us."

"And if we catch him off guard, we just might get him to make a slip or reveal something about what he's up to here. We've already been over this," Joe said impatiently. "Come on, let's get it over with."

"Okay, okay," Frank said. He drew in a deep breath and took in the lush, flowering bushes, the sandy beach below, and the endless pink-streaked sky above. He still wasn't convinced that meeting Kozani head-on was such a smart idea, but Joe was right about one thing—they had to move fast, before whoever planted that spear tried something else. The next time they might not be so lucky. . . .

Kozani's villa came into sight a couple of minutes later. Frank's eyes narrowed when he saw that the door was ajar. A metal cart loaded with cleaning supplies stood on the path just outside. As Frank and Joe moved closer, a cleaning woman came out with a bundle of sheets and towels, which she dumped into a bag.

"Uh-oh," Joe said under his breath. "I don't like the way this looks."

Neither did Frank. He sprinted forward on the path. "Excuse me!" he called out to the cleaning woman. "Miss, could we talk to you for a moment?"

The woman stopped and gave him and Joe a questioning glance. Frank looked past her into the villa, but he didn't see Kozani. "The man who was here, Josef Kozani—did he check out?" he asked the cleaning woman.

"No speaking English," she told them. She started back inside the villa, but Joe stopped her.

"Please. It's important," he urged, but the woman just shrugged.

"Not understanding. New guest," she said.

"New guest," Joe echoed. "That can't be." He stepped around the woman and went into the villa. "Excuse me, ma'am. I just need to use the phone for one second."

The woman followed him inside, speaking angrily in Greek. A minute later she shooed him out of the villa. Then she disappeared back inside and closed the door on them.

"I just called reception," Joe said. "They confirmed it. Kozani checked out and didn't leave a forwarding address."

Frank groaned. "That's just great. So, our top suspect has skipped town, and we don't have a clue where he is. The Gray Man is going to kill us!"

"Wow," Bess said the following morning. She leaned forward in the passenger seat of the rental car that Theo was driving. "Check out the view!"

Looking out the side windows, Nancy saw that the ground to their left dropped off sharply to a narrow valley far below. Winding through the valley was a river surrounded by vineyards and the shimmering dusty green of olive trees. To their right, stony cliffs towered overhead. "Talk about dramatic," she murmured.

There were no hotels at the ancient ruins at Delphi, so they had booked hotel rooms in the small village of Arakhova, nestled into the Parnassos mountains just to the east. Nancy was impatient to get to the museum, but she had to admit that she was glad they decided to leave at five in the morning, rather than at night, so they could enjoy the scenery.

"If you think this is amazing, wait till we get to Delphi," Theo said, glancing at Nancy in the rearview mirror.

Nancy grinned at him. "You sound like you know what you're talking about," she teased. "Are you sure this is your first time to Greece?"

"Definitely," he said, laughing. He patted the guidebook that lay on the seat next to him. "I just happen to be the kind of tourist who always reads up on the places I plan to visit."

After a few more miles, the road wound past one more outcropping, and the ruins of Delphi came into view. Marble columns, temples, statues, and an amphitheater were scattered across a gentle curve of land that dipped between twin cliffs on one side and a high mountaintop on the other. Sunlight reflecting off the cliffs gave a powerful, luminous glow. Below the ancient town, a valley opened into a wide plain carpeted with olive trees and dotted with a few towns. It was one of the most striking sights Nancy had ever seen.

"Unbelievable," Bess said as Theo drove closer to the ruins. "If I had to pick the perfect setting for a spiritual place, this would be it."

"Mmm," Nancy agreed. But then she frowned and added, "I just hope there's nothing sinister going on here. Come on. Let's see what we can find out about the truck that came here from Constantine Shipping."

It took only a few minutes to park in the visitors' lot and get their admission tickets and a map written in English. Nancy, Bess, and Theo opened the map and held it between them. Apart from the ruins, Nancy saw that there was a museum building.

"It says here that the museum houses a collection of art and sculpture from the sanctuaries," she said, reading the blurb on the map. "It makes sense that the truckload from Constantine Shipping would have been delivered there. Mr. Constantine said it was supposed to arrive yesterday evening."

Nancy tucked a strand of flyaway reddish-blond hair behind her ear and started in the direction of the museum with Theo and Bess. A few minutes later a modern building came into sight. A woman wearing a suit was heading toward the entrance ahead of them. When Nancy caught sight of her short black hair and sturdy build, she did a double take.

"You guys!" she hissed, grabbing Bess's arm. "That's Calliope Dalaras!"

"Oh, my gosh—you're right," Bess said. "What's *she* doing here?"

Theo glanced in the older woman's direction. "She's not going into the museum," he whispered. "Should we follow her?"

"Definitely," Nancy and Bess answered at the same time.

Calliope Dalaras wound around the museum to a large, practical-looking stucco building behind it. "Looks like offices or something," Bess said, hesitating. "We're probably not allowed in."

"Since when has that ever stopped us?" Nancy said with a grin.

She was about to head to the entrance when a long cement platform built into the side of the building caught her eye. "Hey, isn't that a loading dock?"

"Looks like it," Theo said, following her gaze.

Changing directions, the three of them hurried around to the platform. Sure enough, there was a wide loading dock. Three metal doors were set into the wall behind it.

"I think we found our way in," Nancy said, nodding at the doors. "Are you two game?"

"What's a little breaking and entering among friends?" Bess said with a nervous laugh.

Theo used a credit card to jimmy the lock. A moment later he, Bess, and Nancy were inside. Nancy closed the door behind them, then looked carefully around.

They were in what looked like a huge storage space. The room's only light came from two small skylights set into the ceiling, but Nancy could still make out marble columns, statues, and pieces of sculpture that filled the space. She didn't hear anything. She hoped that meant they were alone.

"Where do we start?" Theo wanted to know.

"I'm not sure why Alexis's kidnapper would bring her here," Nancy said, thinking out loud. "But it can't hurt to search for any sign of her. Why don't you two look through all this stuff, while I see if I can find a record book. Maybe I can find out where that truck was unloaded."

While Bess and Theo disappeared among the rows of sculptures, Nancy skirted around the outer edge of the storage space. She didn't see an office, but she did spot a closed door set into the far wall. With any luck . . .

Nancy stiffened, hearing a scraping noise just above her head. "What?" She looked up at the heavy marble pedestal to her right. It was about two feet in diameter. A large bust of a woman with flowing marble hair was perched on top of the pedestal and was teetering precariously.

"Oh, no," she said. "It's going to—"

At that moment the bust slipped off the top of the pedestal, right above her head.

Chapter
Eleven

Nancy gasped, leaping back automatically. For the smallest fraction of a second her gaze focused on the statue's face. The expression in the marble eyes was empty as the head plummeted closer.

Crash!

The bust slammed into the cement floor inches from Nancy, breaking into a million sharp bits of stone. Nancy had automatically thrown her arms up in front of her face. The marble debris showered across the floor and pelted her feet and legs.

"Nancy! Theo!" Bess's alarmed voice came from somewhere nearby. "Are you two all right?"

Lowering her arms, Nancy looked down. There was a small cut on her left shin, but otherwise she was unhurt. "Over here," she called out. "I'm fine."

Bess appeared from around the end of the row of statues and columns. Seconds later Theo squeezed between two columns just a few yards from her. Both of them ran toward Nancy, very concerned. "What happened?" Bess asked.

Nancy stared grimly at the marble pedestal the head had been resting on. "Someone pushed a marble bust off the top of that," she said.

"What!" Theo exclaimed. "But who? We're the only ones here."

Nancy blinked, staring at him. "Yes," she said slowly. An idea was just taking shape in her mind, and she didn't like it. Keeping her voice light, she asked, "Where were you two? Did you see or hear anything?"

Bess shook her head. "I was at the other end of the warehouse," she said.

"And I was a couple rows over," Theo added. "I didn't see—" He broke off. "Did you hear that?"

Nancy cocked her head to one side and listened. She heard the muffled sounds of voices outside the door she'd been heading toward. "Someone's coming!"

They raced to the loading dock door, and Nancy cracked it open. "All clear," she said.

The three of them moved quickly and carefully across the loading dock and down the stairs to the ground. "Let's get back to the front before someone sees us and figures out where we've been," Bess urged, anxiously glancing behind her.

Nancy didn't have to be told twice. She started around toward the main entrance, then stopped short. "It's Calliope," she said in a low voice.

The older woman was walking away from the building's entrance. She turned toward them, then paused as her gaze landed on Nancy.

"Uh-oh," Theo whispered. "She sees us."

Calliope's eyes narrowed just the slightest bit. Then she whirled back around and hurried away from them.

"What's her hurry?" Nancy wondered out loud. She started to follow, then hesitated. "I don't want to let her get out of sight, but"—she glanced back at the building Calliope had just left—"I wish we could find out what she was up to. . . ."

Bess pulled on Theo's hand. "Theo and I will see what we can find out back in the building," she assured Nancy. "We'll meet you at the parking lot, okay?"

Nancy gave the thumbs-up sign, then flew down the path Calliope Dalaras had taken. She could see tourists wandering among the temples and in the ancient amphitheater, but Calliope bypassed the ruins. Moving quickly, she exited the museum area and hurried to a sleek sedan in the parking lot. Just before she slipped into the backseat of the car, she glanced over her shoulder at Nancy. Then the door closed and her driver sped away.

Nancy sighed and slowed down. She couldn't just leave Bess and Theo stranded. After walking to their rental car, she leaned against the driver's door and crossed her arms.

Calliope *had* been in the same building as the storage space. Nancy hadn't heard anyone come into the space from the other part of the building, but she supposed it was possible that Calliope had sneaked in somehow and pushed that bust. And the way she'd rushed off just now . . .

"Nancy!" Bess called out. She and Theo were back in the parking lot, walking toward her.

"What happened?" Nancy asked.

Bess grinned at Nancy. "Theo did the talking, since he speaks Greek. He said that we were service representatives of Constantine Shipping, checking to make sure that the truckload of ancient sculpture was delivered to the museum's satisfaction."

"We spoke to the museum's director," Theo added, grinning.

"Did he know about the truck from Constantine Shipping?" Nancy asked.

"Yup," Theo answered. "The sculptures were part of a special exhibit of classical Greek art that traveled abroad. The work is just now being returned to Delphi, and Constantine Shipping was hired to ship it back." He raised an eyebrow at Nancy and added, "The curator said that the sculptures were unloaded last night—into that storage room where we were."

Nancy crossed her arms over her chest, thinking. "So how does Calliope fit into things?" she wondered.

"Actually, I asked the director about her," Theo said. "She's Mr. Constantine's competition, so I pretended to be worried that maybe she was trying to elbow in on Constantine Shipping's business."

"And?" Nancy asked.

"Apparently, that's exactly what she was trying to do," Theo answered, shrugging. "The director wouldn't go into it, but he did say that Calliope had presented him with some kind of business proposal."

Nancy let out a sigh. "That still doesn't tell us anything about Alexis," she said. "We've got to look around here some more."

"Good idea," Theo agreed. "Maybe we'll get lucky and find some clue as to where she is."

"And even if we don't"—Bess turned from Theo to Nancy with a grin—"we'll still get to see one of the most amazing ancient sites in all of Greece!"

Joe leaned forward over the handlebars of the moped that he and Frank were driving to K&B Imports, the company that had hired the two trucks that were blown up. They had called the Gray Man first thing that morning with the news that Josef Kozani had checked out of the Andromeda Palace. The Gray Man hadn't been happy. But he *had* given them some interesting information on K&B Imports. His computer database showed that the company was owned by none other than Josef Kozani. This time, they'd decided to rent a moped rather than take taxis. That way, if anything unexpected happened, they'd at least have a way of making a quick getaway.

"I hope we come up with a solid lead," Joe called over his shoulder to his brother. "We still don't know that Kozani is setting up a deal for Petronia to buy the Phoenix missiles from Terry Brodsky."

"Or that a deal between Brodsky and Petronia even exists," Frank added. "But since Kozani's company rented those two trucks, *and* you thought the missiles could have been on the barge heading to where the trucks were hidden . . ."

"It makes sense that he's involved," Joe finished. "Plus, Kozani was really upset after the trucks exploded. Seems to me that someone else is trying to make sure the Phoenix missiles don't make it to their destination."

"It's an awful lot of 'supposing,' but it all makes some kind of sense—I hope. Now we need proof to back up our theories," Frank said. "It'd be nice to be able to contact the Gray Man with *good* news for a change. I didn't even tell him how scared the staff at the Andromeda Palace is of us after they had to remove that speargun and replace the door."

Joe slowed the moped, looking at the numbers of the buildings they passed. They were in the middle of a run-down industrial neighborhood. The wide road was lined with warehouses, half of which were boarded up or had broken windows. "We're on Iraklidon," he said. "Look for number 173."

"It looks totally deserted around here," Frank commented from behind him.

Joe stopped the moped in front of a dilapidated gray warehouse. The number 173 was written on the door in faded, peeling paint. Half of the windows were broken or missing, and the ones that remained were covered with grime.

"Doesn't exactly look like a thriving business, does it?" he said. "I'd say this place hasn't been used in at least ten years."

"It must be a bogus address," Frank said, frowning. "Whoever hired those trucks from Constantine Shipping didn't want to be traced."

"But if Kozani hired those trucks, why would he use his company's real name? Why not give a phony name along with the phony address?" Joe asked. He checked over his shoulder as he parked the moped in the shadow of the building. Something about the place gave him the creeps. "Unless someone *else* hired the trucks, using K and B Imports instead of their real name."

"Brodsky?" Frank asked.

Joe shrugged. "Maybe. Anyway, as long as we're here, we might as well look inside."

He reached for the doorknob, then stopped, suddenly alert. They'd been so busy talking that he hadn't noticed the door was slightly ajar. "It's probably just some local kids who broke in," he said, shaking himself. But as they stepped inside, he moved with extra caution.

The area just inside the door was blocked by a tall pyramid of caved-in cardboard boxes. As Joe skirted around them, he saw a small office. Glass panes had once covered the top half of the walls, but they had been knocked out long ago. Dusty shards of glass were scattered across the floor. They looked as if they hadn't been disturbed in years. Beyond the office was a huge open work space. Shafts of glaring sun shone through the broken windows, breaking up the shadowy gloom.

Joe was just a step from the office when he caught sight of some movement among the shadows at the far end of the warehouse. Someone was there!

As the person moved into a shaft of light, Joe

could make out the man's tall, muscular body, hair, and intense, angular face. Joe's mouth dropped open. He'd seen that man before, staring back at him from one of the photos in their background file.

It was Terry Brodsky!

Chapter

Twelve

FRANK WAS just stepping around the pile of cardboard boxes when he spotted Brodsky at the far end of the warehouse.

Whoa! What's *he* doing here? Frank thought, ducking back behind the boxes. When he looked up again, he saw that Joe was crouched inside a separate office with its windows completely broken out. Joe met his gaze and put a finger silently to his lips before turning back in Brodsky's direction.

Frank didn't let himself budge. Luckily, the warehouse was huge. Brodsky had to be over a hundred feet from them. But he also happened to be highly trained in undercover operations. If Brodsky spotted them, Frank didn't want to think what might happen. . . .

Taking a deep breath, Frank peered around the boxes. So far, so good. Brodsky didn't appear to have seen or heard them. He was walking through the open warehouse, stopping every now and then to poke into a corner or a box. What was going on? Frank wondered. Brodsky didn't seem to be any more familiar with the warehouse than he and Joe.

After a few minutes Brodsky appeared to be done and was starting back toward the door. Frank stiffened and ducked back behind the boxes. He could hear Brodsky's footsteps moving closer. Suddenly the scuffing sounds stopped. Frank froze. His heart pounded against the inside of his rib cage. Does he know we're here? he wondered.

The silence seemed to stretch forever. Then the footsteps abruptly resumed. A second later Frank heard the warehouse door open and shut.

When he peered around the boxes again, the only person he saw was Joe. "Talk about a close call!" Joe whispered.

Frank nodded. He pushed himself to standing and quickly headed for the door. "We can pat ourselves on the back later," he said urgently. "We may have lost Kozani's trail, but we're not going to lose Brodsky's. Come on!"

"I can't believe it," Bess said early Friday evening. "We've been to Delphi and back, said goodbye to Theo, *and* driven back here to Constantine Shipping"—she turned in the passenger seat of their rental car to look at Nancy—"all before dinner time."

"Too bad we weren't able to come up with any more clues as to where Alexis is being held," Nancy said, frowning. "I feel as if we're letting Mr. Constantine down."

She stopped the car at the Constantine Shipping security gate. The guard checked their names on a list and waved them through. "I'm sorry you didn't have a chance to see more of Theo," Nancy said.

"That's okay," Bess said with a sad smile. "I mean, he's a great guy, but I'd feel terrible if we didn't do everything we could to find Alexis."

"Mmm." Nancy felt badly for Bess, but she had to admit she was relieved that Theo was gone. There had been a lingering suspicion in her mind ever since that marble bust had come so close to hitting her. Could Theo have pushed it? She didn't know why he would, or how he could be involved in Alexis's kidnapping. But he *had* been in the warehouse.

Nancy shook herself, pulling the car to a stop in front of the *Island Princess*.

"Nancy! Bess!" Mr. Constantine's deep voice called out from the yacht as the two girls got out of the car. He was standing next to the rail, with Petros beside him. "At last you are back!"

His tone was so urgent that Nancy knew that something had happened. "Did you hear from the kidnappers?" she asked as she and Bess hurried up the ramp to the deck.

Alexis's father nodded. "I think it was a man speaking," he said. "He told me that I must pay one million U.S. dollars to get my daughter back."

"Did they arrange for a time and place to pay the money and get Alexis?" Nancy asked.

"Yes," Mr. Constantine answered, nodding. "At eight o'clock tonight. I must leave the money in a briefcase beneath the mosaic of the Virgin Mary at the monastery of Daphni—"

"A Byzantine church outside of Athens," Petros explained. "It dates from the sixth century."

"Yes, yes," Mr. Constantine said impatiently. "After I leave the money, I am to return here to the yacht. Then the kidnappers will contact me and tell me where I can find Alexis."

Bess looked worriedly at Nancy, biting her lower lip. "But what if they just take the money and run? How can you be sure they'll release Alexis?"

"I *cannot* be sure, but I have no choice. If I do not do as they say, they will kill her." Mr. Constantine let out a heavy sigh and leaned against the yacht's railing. "I have already gotten the money. It is in my safe here on the yacht. The kidnappers warned me again against telling the police. Only Captain Costas, my first captain, knows what has happened. I thought he should be aware, in case we need to take the *Island Princess* to pick up Alexis. I gave the rest of the yacht's staff time off."

"Does the monastery have a place where Bess and I could hide?" Nancy asked. "We could follow whoever picks up the money. Let's hope the kidnappers will let Alexis go. But if not . . ."

"Then we still have a chance of getting her back alive," Mr. Constantine finished thoughtfully.

"I do not think we should take a chance," Petros said firmly. "I will go alone to leave the money, as we discussed."

"You're already taking a chance," Nancy pointed out. "Bess and I will be practically invisible, I promise. If we travel there separately, there's no reason for the kidnappers to suspect anything."

Mr. Constantine's steady brown eyes swept over the dock areas. "Nancy and Bess shall go, too."

Petros didn't say anything more, but as they all went inside the yacht, Nancy felt his cold, hard eyes boring into her back.

"Is Brodsky *ever* going to come out of there?" Joe whispered to his brother. "My knees hurt from hiding here so long."

"Not to mention that we could be in serious

hot water if the Constantine Shipping security guards decide to check this area," Frank added.

He and Frank were hunched down behind some kind of storage shed outside the main Constantine Shipping office. From what Joe could tell, it was a no-man's-land between the back of the offices and the dock facilities. All Joe could see were a few storage sheds, a Dumpster heaped with waste, and a metal building with dozens of wires leading to and from it. It wasn't scenic, but if Terry Brodsky was interested in checking it out, then so were he and Frank.

After leaving the deserted warehouse, Brodsky led them straight to Constantine Shipping. Joe hadn't been surprised when the ex-operative cut a hole in the chain-link fence instead of stopping at security. Brodsky then headed straight for the electrical building. He'd been inside ever since.

"What's he up to?" Joe said impatiently.

Frank's gaze didn't budge from the metal building where Brodsky was. "With all those wires, I'd say that has to be the power center for the shipping complex. Maybe the communications center, too."

"But what does that have to do with the Phoenix missiles?" Joe asked.

"I have no idea. Maybe he's trying to sabotage Constantine's security system," Frank said. "Why, I don't know."

Just then Joe spotted a flicker of movement at the power center. "He's out," he whispered.

Brodsky was outside and looking furtively around. He held something, Joe saw. A headset with wires attached. "Maybe he *was* interested in the communications center," he said. "Doesn't that look like phone-tapping equipment?"

Frank nodded, ducking farther behind the storage shed. "He's heading back this way."

The Hardys followed at a distance as Brodsky left the shipping compound through the hole he'd cut in the fence. His motorcycle was hidden in the brush just outside. As soon as he started the motor and drove off, Joe jumped to get their moped from behind some flowering bushes.

"He's taking the road that goes back toward Athens," Frank said, hopping on the moped behind Joe. "Don't lose him!"

Joe had to wind through traffic in order to keep Brodsky's motorcycle in sight. After about ten minutes Brodsky turned off the main road and headed north, and then east, away from the city. At last, he stopped at an old-looking church. Joe noticed that Brodsky parked his moped in an inconspicuous spot across the street instead of using the parking lot.

Joe held back a few hundred yards and cut the motor of their moped. Brodsky stayed in view only for a moment before walking quickly toward the church. Leaving their moped at the side of the road, Joe and Frank crept over to a bank of azaleas that lined the street in front of the church. In the deepening twilight, Joe couldn't see all the details, but the old stone church looked as if it had been standing for many centuries.

"There he is," Frank whispered, pointing toward some olive trees.

Sure enough, Brodsky's powerful silhouette was just visible in the shadows. "What's your game, Brodsky?" Joe wondered out loud.

He let his eyes play over the grounds. The small parking lot outside the church held only one car, but a dark sedan was just pulling in. Joe was surprised when he saw Petros Apollonious get out of the sedan carrying a briefcase. Petros looked left and right before walking inside the church.

"What's *he* doing here?" Joe whispered.

Frank shrugged, keeping his gaze on the church entrance. The door opened again a few moments later, and Petros came back out of the church. "He's out again—minus the briefcase," Frank whispered. He watched while Petros returned to his car and drove away. "I don't get it," he added. "Do you think he just dropped off money for Alexis's kidnappers?"

"It makes sense, except . . ." Joe's eyes flitted to the trees where Brodsky was. "Why would *Brodsky* be interested in that?"

Frank shrugged. "Maybe it's a coincidence that they're both here. All I know is that Petros wasn't in there long enough to do much praying." He looked at the parking lot again. "Looks like we've got another visitor."

A beat-up truck was pulling into the lot. Joe peered at the squat, barrel-chested man who got out and headed toward the church. Something about him was familiar, but Joe couldn't place it. "I know I've seen that guy. . . ."

Just then the man stepped up to the heavy wooden doors, and an outside light illuminated his face and bare arms. Joe was startled when he caught sight of the tattoo on the man's arm. "That's the guy from the barge!" he whispered. "The one I saw right before the trucks were blown up the other night."

"What!" Frank whipped his head around to stare at the man, who was just disappearing inside the church. "I wish we could get in there."

"Too obvious. We'll have to wait," Joe said, his voice low. He glanced back at the olive trees, but there wasn't any activity. "Looks like Brodsky's waiting, too."

"I wish I knew how he fits into all of this. . . ." Frank whispered. His voice trailed off and his body tensed up. "The guy with the tattoo is coming out again—and guess what he's carrying?"

Joe had already spotted the briefcase the man held. He crouched, his senses on red-alert. "Get ready to rock 'n' roll," he whispered.

The man with the tattoo walked very quickly

back to his pickup truck, checking over his shoulder twice. "He doesn't look like he's going to waste any time getting out of here," Frank said. "One of us better stay on him."

"I'm on it," Joe volunteered. "You stick around here to see what Brodsky's up to. We'll meet back at the resort later."

Joe was about to head off for the moped when a movement in the olive trees made him stop. "Brodsky's making a move!" he whispered.

Brodsky was off like a shot. His dark shadow raced from tree to tree, heading toward the parking lot. The man with the tattoo was just starting his truck. As the truck pulled away, Brodsky leaped and landed on the truck bed.

"They're making a getaway!" Frank cried in dismay. "Come on!"

Chapter

Thirteen

FOR THE LAST HALF HOUR Nancy and Bess had been slumped down in the front seat of their rental car, watching the church at the monastery of Daphni. Finally the girls spotted a heavyset man leave the church and start up a pickup truck. As Nancy got ready to follow, another man darted out from some olive trees and ran over to the truck.

Nancy turned the key in the ignition of the rental car. "Maybe he's some kind of lookout," she guessed. "We have to follow them."

The truck turned left and headed east, away from Athens. Nancy was just pulling out after it, when she spotted two *more* people next to the shrubs in front of the church. "It's Frank and Joe!"

"What are *they* doing here?" Bess asked, totally confused.

"There's one way to find out," Nancy said. She peeled out of the parking lot and stopped the car right in front of the Hardys. Both boys' mouths dropped open when they saw Nancy and Bess.

"Just get in!" Nancy urged, reaching around her seat back to flip open the rear door. "We'll talk while we drive."

Frank and Joe dove in, pulling the door shut behind them. "Terry Brodsky's on the back of that truck," Joe said.

"Brodsky?" Nancy said. She felt as if she were watching a film on fast forward and couldn't keep the story straight.

Ahead of them the pickup truck suddenly gathered speed, fishtailing around a curve in the road. Terry Brodsky was crouched in the open truck bed, hanging on to a side. "Uh-oh, I think they've spotted us," Frank said. "Don't lose them!"

Nancy raced after the truck. "What's Brodsky doing mixed up in all of this?"

"That's what we're hoping to find out," Joe answered, bracing himself against the car door.

Up ahead, the truck was heading around a hairpin curve. "Hang on to your hats, guys!" Nancy called.

She didn't have time to slow down before they went shooting into the sharp curve. Her heart leaped into her throat as the car tipped dangerously on two wheels before righting itself.

"That was close," Bess said in a high voice.

To their right the ground sloped sharply downward. In a dizzying glance, Nancy saw moonlight glimmering on water below and a ribbon of road that twisted toward it down the hill. "They're heading for the gulf," she realized. "I just hope we all make it down there in one piece!"

The truck was careening around the next curve now. The driver didn't seem to care how fast he took the turns, but Nancy wasn't about to send everyone in her car flying off the side of the road.

"They can't get *that* far ahead," Frank said under his breath. "Not without killing themselves."

Finally the road flattened out into a modern causeway that stretched across a marshy area leading to the Saronic Gulf. "There!" Joe called out, pointing.

The truck's rear lights were two tiny pinpoints about half a mile ahead of them on the causeway. Nancy poured on more speed, trying to draw closer. Beyond the truck she could make out the twinkling lights of some buildings.

"Looks like a port," Joe said. He'd pulled some binoculars from his belt pack and was peering through them. "Hey! They're stopping!"

Nancy turned off the causeway onto a short road leading to the port. They found the pickup parked in front of some buildings next to a pier. She could just make out the driver's squat silhouette running toward the water. Brodsky had jumped off the truck and was following.

"Come on!" Nancy urged her car forward, but they were still fifty yards away. The shorter guy was just starting up a speedboat that was tied to the pier. In a second they'd be gone!

"What?" Joe murmured, still staring through his binoculars. "Brodsky and that other guy are struggling. Whoa! Brodsky just yanked the briefcase from the tattooed guy's hand. Now he's getting *off* the boat!"

Nancy had to watch the road, but she thought she saw Brodsky dart toward the buildings next to the pier. Seconds later she ground the rental car to a stop right behind the pickup truck. Frank and Joe flew out the back doors, heading for Brodsky.

"The boat!" Nancy cried. As she jumped out, the speedboat was already pulling away from the pier. All she could do was watch in frustration as it buzzed out of sight on the water.

Nancy whirled around to the boxlike buildings clustered next to the pier. Frank and Joe were just emerging from an alleyway that ran between two of them. "No luck?" Nancy guessed.

Joe shook his head. "Brodsky *and* the money are gone."

"What are we going to do!" Bess asked, leaning against the car door.

"For starters, I think we should try to figure out what just happened," Frank said. "I don't know about the rest of you, but I'm totally confused about how all of us ended up chasing the same people."

Nancy nodded. "That makes two of us. What was Brodsky doing with the man who picked up the kidnapper's money?" she asked.

"Not to mention that the guy just happens to be the same person I saw the other night," Joe said. "He was on a barge heading right for the shore, just before the trucks blew up at the Andromeda Palace."

"Didn't you tell us you thought that barge might be carrying the Phoenix missiles?" Bess asked. When Joe nodded, she said, "I'm *totally* confused. Are you guys saying that Brodsky is involved with the stolen missiles *and* Alexis's kidnapping?"

"Looks that way," Frank replied. "I know it seems crazy, but after what just happened I think our cases must be linked."

Nancy stared out over the water, thinking. "Until now, all the clues we've come up with point to either Calliope Dalaras or Petros as the kidnapper," she said. "They each had a motive and were on the scene when Alexis disappeared. I don't get how Brodsky or that other guy could have gotten to Alexis."

"Brodsky seems to know his way around Constantine Shipping," Frank said. "We followed him there earlier today, and he sneaked in and out without security ever spotting him."

"Or us," Joe added with a cocky smile.

"There's something else I don't get," Frank added slowly. "The way Brodsky yanked the briefcase away from the other man didn't seem exactly friendly. And then they disappeared in different directions. If they're working together, why wouldn't both of them go in the speedboat?"

Nancy's head was starting to ache from so many questions. "Let's search the truck," she suggested. "Maybe we'll find something there."

"Good idea," Joe agreed. He and Frank hopped into the front, so Nancy climbed up on the rear bumper and leaned into the open truck bed. She checked it out and found it was completely empty.

"Nothing here," she told Bess, hopping to the ground. They headed to the front of the truck just as Joe leaped out of the passenger side.

"Check it out," he said, waving a crinkled paper at them. "I found this in the glove compartment."

Taking the paper, Nancy saw that it was a map of Greece. "The island of Crete's been circled," she said, tracing the pen mark with her finger. "And a town's been marked with an *X*."

"Chania," Joe supplied. "Which happens to be exactly where Sofia Alcalay went."

"Do you think Alexis's kidnappers took her there?" Bess asked. "I mean, why go so far away?"

"Ditto about the missiles," Joe said. "If they're headed for Petronia, it doesn't make sense to take them in the exact opposite direction."

Frank stepped over to them from the driver's side of the cab. "I don't know what's up," he said, "but I think Joe and I had better head to Crete."

"I wish we could go," Nancy said. "But we have to report to Mr. Constantine and Petros."

"I'll tell you what," Joe said. "If we find any clue to where Alexis is, we'll contact you on the Constantines' yacht. All we ask in return is one tiny little favor."

"What's that?" Nancy asked, arching her brow.

"A ride back to our moped?" Joe said, grinning. "It's back at that monastery."

Nancy couldn't help grinning back. "I think we can handle that," she told him.

When Nancy and Bess returned to the *Island Princess,* Mr. Constantine and Petros Apollonious were both in the steering house. Captain Costas, a slender man with warm brown eyes and graying dark hair, was with them.

"Thank goodness you are safe!" Alexis's father cried, rushing over to the girls. "You were gone so long that Petros and I were starting to worry."

Leaving Captain Costas in the steering house, he and Petros ushered the two girls down the stairs to the yacht's living room. Before they even sat down, Alexis's father asked, "Did you see who picked up the money? Were you able to follow them?"

"Well . . ." Nancy exchanged a quick look with Bess. "Things didn't go exactly the way we planned."

"No?" Petros asked. His dark eyes flicked nervously back and forth between Nancy and Bess.

Nancy and Bess took turns explaining what had happened at the monastery of Daphni and during the chase that followed. "We did everything we could, but Terry Brodsky and the other guy both got away," Nancy finished.

"With the money," Bess added quietly. "Sorry. I know we let you down."

Mr. Constantine didn't say anything, but Nancy could read the worry in his eyes. He had aged years in just the past few minutes.

"I knew it was a mistake for you to go!" Petros burst out angrily. "You have probably ruined our chances of ever seeing Alexis alive again!"

"Petros," Mr. Constantine said, waving a hand to silence him. "Nancy and Bess have done their best to help us. All we can do now is wait for the kidnappers to call." He gave a wry smile, then said, "When they do, we may have another way to find out where these people are holding my daughter."

"What are you talking about?" Bess asked.

Mr. Constantine gestured to the phone that sat on the living room's coffee table. An electronic device that looked something like an answering machine was hooked up to it.

"You're going to trace the call?" Nancy guessed.

Alexis's father nodded. "I cannot stand by and do nothing, when these people hold my daughter's life in their hands," he said firmly. "My chief of security installed this tracking device. He is monitoring from the security booth outside."

Nancy eyed the weatherproof cable that snaked away from the phone and disappeared out of one of the yacht's high windows. It looked like some kind of electrical hookup, but Nancy wasn't sure why Mr. Constantine would need it. "Don't most boats use cellular phones?" she asked.

"Yes, but both times the kidnapper called, he used the office telephone number to contact me. This cord connects to a dockside telephone jack, so that I can take the call here instead," Mr. Constantine explained. "If we can keep the caller on the line for just thirty seconds, we will be able to tell from what location he is calling."

At that moment the ringer on the phone sounded. Nancy caught the determination on Mr. Constantine's face as he flicked on the tracking device, then grabbed the phone and answered it. Nancy checked her watch and started counting.

A moment later Mr. Constantine gave a nod. It

was the kidnappers! Alexis's father's tone was pleading. Nancy didn't understand the Greek words, but she had a feeling the kidnappers were giving him a hard time about being followed from the monastery of Daphni.

When she checked her watch again, her heart started beating faster. If he could just keep the person on the line for another ten seconds . . .

Suddenly Mr. Constantine broke off in the middle of a sentence. He shook the phone and muttered something in Greek.

Nancy felt a knot of dread twist in her stomach.

Mr. Constantine said simply, "The line went dead!"

Chapter

Fourteen

Nancy could hardly believe what she'd heard. "No!" she cried automatically.

"Perhaps there was enough time," Mr. Constantine asked hopefully. He slammed down the phone and ran up the steps to the deck. When he came back a few minutes later, he was frowning. "The trace did not go through," he told them.

"I'm sorry," Nancy said.

Petros walked over to his boss and clapped an arm around his shoulders. "We may have better luck when they call again," he said.

Something about the tone of Petros's voice made Nancy give him a sideways glance. Despite his consoling words, Petros seemed more relieved than upset. And the way his dark eyes shifted . . .

"How could the phone just go dead like that?" Nancy wondered out loud. "It's not as if there's a storm or anything that could knock out the line."

"Perhaps the kidnapper simply hung up," Petros suggested.

Mr. Constantine shook his head. "We were in the middle of speaking. The man was furious. He said that we took the money from him. Now the deal is off. He refuses to let Alexis go free."

"Oh, no," Bess murmured.

Nancy remembered what Joe had said about Brodsky taking the briefcase from the other person by force. So maybe Brodsky *wasn't* in on the kidnapping.

"I said I would pay more money," Mr. Constantine went on. "The man was listening, but then . . . the line went dead."

"There must be some explanation," Nancy said, looking more closely at the phone. She wasn't sure, but the cord that connected it to the dock seemed to hang with a little more slack than before. "Where, exactly, does this cord go?"

"Come. I will show you," Mr. Constantine offered.

He led the way up through the steering house, where Captain Costas was reading a newspaper. Mr. Constantine spoke to him sharply, and the captain jumped to his feet. After muttering something in rapid-fire Greek, the captain rushed out to the deck and down the ramp to the dock.

The rest of the group followed him to a square

post that was dotted with electrical outlets. Nancy's gaze followed the cable that stretched from the yacht to the electrical hookup. "It's been disconnected," she said.

Mr. Constantine, Petros, and Captain Costas were all speaking Greek. Nancy didn't need to understand their words to know that they were upset. Seconds later Petros and Captain Costas strode away, heading toward a small wooden building about twenty yards down the dock.

"They are going to find out from my head of security how this could have happened," Mr. Constantine told Nancy and Bess, shaking his head. "Such a lapse of security is unacceptable."

Nancy followed Petros with her eyes before turning to follow Mr. Constantine back onto the *Island Princess*. Petros could have pulled the cable loose from inside the yacht, she decided. She hadn't actually seen him pull the cord, but he could have.

Until now she'd kept her thoughts about Petros quiet. But if he was sabotaging their efforts to get Alexis back, Nancy thought, Mr. Constantine needed to know about her suspicions.

As soon as they were on board the yacht and settled in the living room, Nancy turned to him. "I'm not sure how to tell you this," she began. "But I think that Petros might be involved in Alexis's kidnapping.

The older man swiveled toward her. "Petros? That is impossible!"

Taking turns, the two girls told Mr. Constantine about the threat Petros had made to Alexis in the café. They also reminded Mr. Constantine that Petros had left the shipping office just before Alexis disappeared.

"It is not unusual for Petros to leave the office," Mr. Constantine said when they were done. "He likes to personally oversee the details of my business."

Or personally oversee Alexis's kidnapping, Nancy added to herself. Aloud, she just said, "What about his promise to kill Alexis?"

Alexis's father gave a dismissive wave of his hand. "Perhaps your friend's Greek is not as good as he pretends. Even if Petros *did* say something, I am sure he didn't mean it. He *was* upset after Alexis broke off their engagement, but he would never harm her. I am sure of it," he insisted. "What about the attack at Spetses? That must have been the kidnappers' first attempt, but Petros could not have been responsible. He was in the office working."

"The first attack could have been made by an accomplice, the man who picked up the money," Nancy said.

"This man could just as easily be working for Calliope Dalaras," Mr. Constantine pointed out. "She, too, was at the office when Alexis disappeared, *and* you saw her at Delphi, did you not?"

Nancy nodded. She wasn't surprised that Mr. Constantine was sticking up for Petros, but she wanted to make sure he knew all the facts. "Did you notice how Petros was really against the idea of Bess and me going to the monastery? It was as if he didn't want us to find out who the kidnappers were. And just now . . . well, he could have pulled the phone line loose so that the trace couldn't go through."

Mr. Constantine sat on the living room couch and crossed his arms over his chest. "I am telling you, Petros would never do such a thing to Alexis and me," he repeated. "I trust him. Our families have known each other for many years." He looked directly at Nancy. "I do not question his loyalty."

"I'm not saying that Petros is definitely involved," Nancy said. "Just that he might be." Mr. Constantine obviously wasn't going to be swayed. "Anyway, I guess what we really need to concentrate on is what to do next."

He nodded. "I have been thinking, I must stay here until the kidnappers contact me again," he said slowly. "But if they are taking my daughter to Crete, I would like to have someone nearby."

"Do you want Bess and me to go?" Nancy asked.

"You will go with Petros," Mr. Constantine said firmly. "Captain Costas will take you to

Chania. And if you find nothing, then you will proceed to our home on Kiros."

"That makes sense," Bess said, nodding. "Then, if anything happens there, at least we won't be as far away as if we had *all* stayed here in Piraeus."

It sounded like a solid plan. The only thing Nancy wasn't crazy about was that Petros would be with them. Even if Mr. Constantine trusted him, she didn't. From the moment we leave here, I'm going to keep a close eye on Petros, she said to herself.

Frank Hardy paused on the wide, cobbled street that curved around the crescent-shaped waterfront of Chania, on the coast of Crete. "This may be the most frustrating case we've ever been on," he said, "but at least the scenery is decent."

It was Saturday afternoon, and a few brightly colored fishing boats were just coming into the harbor. Venetian-style buildings ringed the waterfront. Behind them, narrow cobbled lanes rose gradually up into the hills.

"Frustrating? What are you talking about, Frank?" Joe shoved his hands into his shorts pockets, peering out at the deep blue water. "All we have to do is find Terry Brodsky and the guy with the tattoo and recover the Phoenix missiles—"

"Don't forget Sofia Alcalay," Frank added.

"We have to find her, too, and figure out how she plays into all of this."

Joe shrugged and grinned at Frank. "Piece of cake. We'll have this case solved and be on a plane back to the States by tonight."

"In your dreams," Frank said, rolling his eyes. He quickly checked his watch, then groaned. "We've already wasted half the day finding a hotel room—"

He broke off, his eyes focusing on a dark-haired girl in a white dress who was just coming out of the hotel right next to them. "I think we just got our first break, Joe," he said, his voice low.

Joe followed Frank's gaze, then blinked in surprise. "Sofia! See, I told you this would be a breeze." He loped toward Sofia, calling her name.

For half a second she acted completely stunned—and anything but happy. But Frank had to hand it to her, she recovered almost immediately. "Joe! Frank!" she said, plastering a bright smile on her face. "I am so glad to see you! What a surprise!"

I'll bet, Frank thought to himself. Aloud, he just said, "I didn't know you were coming to Crete. I guess you finished all that *schoolwork*, huh."

"Oh—that . . ." Sofia let out a laugh that sounded a little too bright. "With so much work, I needed to take a break."

While she spoke she slipped her room key into her bag, but not before Frank caught a glimpse of the number 7 printed on the tag. He eyed the entrance to her hotel. If Joe could just keep Sofia busy, he could sneak in and search her room.

"Hey, Sofia," Joe said, breaking into Frank's thoughts. "Why don't you and I get something to drink at one of these cafés?"

He caught Frank's eye and gave an imperceptible nod to the hotel. Obviously, Joe had seen the key, too, and guessed what Frank was thinking. Way to go, brother, Frank congratulated him silently.

"I don't know if I should—" Sofia began, but Frank wasn't about to let her go that easily.

"Sure you can," he insisted. "You're on vacation, right? You can do what you want."

Sofia was about to object, but Joe was already steering her toward the other end of the waterfront. "I'll see you in a minute," Frank said. "I've got to get my, uh, camera."

As soon as their backs were turned, Frank slipped into the doorway he'd seen Sofia leave. He found himself in a courtyard filled with potted flowers and trees. The hotel rooms ran around the courtyard on two levels. Through an arched doorway to his left Frank spotted a middle-aged woman standing behind a reception desk. Slipping quietly past the doorway, Frank headed for the first-floor rooms.

Room 7 was at the rear of the courtyard,

behind a huge potted palm. Not bad, Frank thought. I ought to be able to get in and out without attracting any attention.

He skirted quietly around a room service tray that had been left outside Room 6, then reached for the door to Sofia's room.

Hey, he thought, stopping in midstride. The door to Room 7 was slightly ajar. Sofia hadn't said anything about traveling with anyone else, but he could hear a person moving around inside her room.

Taking a deep breath, Frank tiptoed the last few steps to the door and peered in through the crack. He caught sight of a sliver of bed with a suitcase open on it. Someone was bent over it. A man—with his back was to Frank. All Frank could see was short dark hair and a lightweight shirt and slacks.

Frank watched silently as the man slid his hands into the suitcase and rummaged around. Why was this guy so interested in Sofia? Just then the man turned, and Frank could make out his well-trimmed beard in profile.

Whoa! Frank thought, moving away from the door. It was Josef Kozani!

Chapter

Fifteen

FRANK'S BRAIN went into overdrive. What was going on? He'd thought that Kozani might be working with Sofia to buy the Phoenix missiles. But if that were true, why would he have to sneak around behind her back?

Frank didn't know what, if anything, Kozani had found. But he wanted to make sure the businessman didn't leave Sofia's room with any clue that could help him and Joe find the missiles and Brodsky.

Out of the corner of his eye Frank spotted the room service tray that had been left outside the next room. It held only two crumpled-up cloth napkins and a few scraps of leftover bread. . . . Still, Kozani didn't have to know that.

Frank grabbed one of the napkins and spread it out over the plate. Then, holding the tray up as if he were delivering a fresh meal, he knocked loudly on the door and pushed it open.

"Kalimera!" he said, flashing Kozani a bright smile. He thought he remembered that that was the traditional Greek greeting.

Kozani straightened up with a gasp and whirled around to face Frank. His beady eyes flashed to Frank's face and then to the tray in his hands. Frank had acted so quickly, he hadn't thought about what he would do if Kozani spoke to him in Greek. Luckily, the businessman seemed flustered at having been caught. While Frank put the tray down on Sofia's dresser, Josef Kozani mumbled something and gave Frank a crisp nod before walking out through the open door.

Frank waited until he saw Kozani disappear through the hotel entrance, then he ducked back into Sofia's room and closed the door. Quickly, he went to the dresser and closet, but both were empty. Apparently, Sofia hadn't bothered to unpack yet. There were some toiletries on the dresser top, but Frank decided to start with the suitcase on the bed. He slipped his hands among the shirts, shorts, and dresses, but didn't find anything suspicious.

He was about to shut the suitcase when something about it caught his attention. Was it his imagination, or was the nylon of the top panel thicker than on the rest of the bag? It was almost as if there were more than one layer.

Flipping the top up again, Frank felt carefully around the edges. About halfway around, his finger slipped beneath a loose edge. He gave a gentle tug and then heard a soft rip as a Velcro closing released. Yes! There *was* a secret flap. The opening was just about large enough for him to slip his hand in.

Seconds later Frank pulled out a flat passport from Petronia. He opened it, and sure enough, there was Sofia's photograph. But when he glanced over at the information listed opposite the photo, he let out a low whistle.

"Sofia *Dvorniak,* huh?" he muttered.

He tapped his fingers against the photo, turning the new name over in his mind. *Dvorniak* . . . It sounded familiar, but he couldn't recall where he'd heard the name before. Was it an alias? Maybe *Alcalay* was a phony name she'd been using, so that he and Joe wouldn't know her real name. Either way, the fact that she was using two names gave Frank yet another reason to suspect her.

As he turned to the next page of the passport, a stub of cardboard fell onto the bed. Picking it up, Frank saw that it was a bus ticket. Luckily, the destination was written in the Roman alphabet as well as in Greek symbols. "Chora Sfakion," Frank read aloud. The date stamped on the ticket was the next day.

The sound of voices in the courtyard reminded Frank that he needed to hurry. He quickly shoved the ticket back between the passport's pages, then slid the tiny book back into its hiding place. A hurried search through the rest of the room turned up nothing else. After checking to make sure everything was the way he'd found it, Frank grabbed the room service tray and stepped out of the room. He returned the tray to its spot outside Room 6, then left the hotel.

Outside, the hot afternoon sunshine danced on the Aegean and shone brightly on the restaurants along the waterfront. Glancing at his watch, Frank saw that it had been about fifteen minutes since he'd left Joe and Sofia. If he didn't get back to them soon, Sofia might start to get suspicious.

He had already taken a few steps toward the café when he spotted an outdoor vendor with postcards, T-shirts, and disposable cameras. "I'll take one of those," he said, pointing to a camera.

A minute later he was jogging toward the café where Joe and Sofia had gone. He spotted them sipping cold drinks at an outside table, beneath a blue- and white-striped awning. When Frank was just a few yards away, he stopped and held up the camera.

"Smile!" he called out, snapping the photo as they both turned his way. Even through the tiny viewfinder he could see the strained and impatient expression on Sofia's face.

"I really must go now," she said.

"So soon?" Joe objected as Frank gave him a thumbs-up.

"I have arranged for a tour of the fortress," Sofia said, nodding toward a series of high stone walls overlooking Chania to the west. "I must go now, or . . ." Her voice trailed off as she eyed the cardboard casing of Frank's disposable camera. "You did not bring your *own* camera on vacation?"

Frank held up his hands helplessly. "I always seem to forget something when I go away."

Sofia nodded distractedly. Slinging the strap of her bag over her shoulder, she got to her feet. "Well, I hope we'll see one another again."

This time Joe didn't object. He and Frank waved goodbye, and Sofia continued west on the road that led to the fort. As soon as she was gone, Frank told Joe about surprising Josef Kozani in her hotel room, and about the passport and bus ticket he'd found.

"Wait a minute," Joe said, his brow furrowed. "First we see Kozani and Sofia acting like buddies in a café in Athens. I mean, if they *are* working together to get the Phoenix missiles from Terry Brodsky, why would Kozani be sneaking around in Sofia's room here in Crete?"

"Good question," Frank told him. "One thing's for sure. If Sofia's using an alias, she's definitely up to something."

"Dvorniak, huh?" Joe said, finishing his iced tea. "You know, that name sounds familiar. I'm sure it was in our file." Suddenly he snapped his fingers. "The Petronian ambassador to Greece—isn't his last name Dvorniak?"

It sounded right to Frank. "We can check our file back at the hotel. Do you think Sofia's handling the secret negotiations to buy the Phoenix missiles?"

Joe shrugged. "Her father's a pretty high-profile figure in Athens. He must have known that the U.S. would be keeping their eye on him once the Phoenix missiles were stolen. But who would suspect a cute girl like Sofia?"

"You sure didn't," Frank pointed out, shooting his brother a sideways grin. "Anyway, I say we head to the bus station and get tickets to Chora Sfakion, wherever that is. If we can find out what Sofia's up to there, our luck on this case might finally turn around."

"Talk about bad luck!" Frank said with a groan the following morning. "I mean, not only was the bus to Chora Sfakion totally booked, but now we're stuck hiking ten miles through a gorge to get there."

Joe nodded, trying to put a lid on his own frustration. He and Frank had found out that Chora Sfakion was a small port town on the southern coast of Crete. But getting there was turning out to be a huge ordeal. The buses were completely booked for the next two days. He and Frank hadn't even been able to get a rental car.

Trying to solve their case at the height of the tourist season definitely had its problems.

Finally a man selling tickets at the Chania bus station had come up with a solution. He was able to find the Hardys seats on a bus heading south, to a town at the northern end of a place called the Samaria Gorge. They'd made the trip early that morning. But they still had to hike through the gorge to Crete's southern coast and then take a short ferry ride to Chora Sfakion.

Joe stared out at the gorge, which dropped down in a steep curve from the high plain where he and Frank stood. A rugged path zigzagged down to the floor of the gorge. Joe spotted gnarled tree roots, rocks, and vines that barely clung to the steep sides. "Looks like pretty rough going," he said, frowning. "How long did the guy at the bus station say it would take us?"

"Six hours. Maybe longer," Frank answered.

"We might as well get started, then." Joe shouldered his backpack, then headed for the start of the trail.

It was slow going at first. He and Frank both tripped over roots and rocks on the steep path. "After all this, Sofia better still be in Chora Sfakion when we get there," Joe said.

"At least now we have a motive for her being involved in acquiring the Phoenix missiles," Frank said from behind him. "We should keep an eye out for both her and the guy with the tattoo."

Joe nodded. "And Brodsky. He'll have to surface somewhere if he wants to sell the missiles. . . ."

He stopped suddenly on the path, cocking his head to one side. "I thought I heard something moving in the brush off the path," he whispered.

He and Frank stood completely still. Joe scoured the steep hillside, but saw only rocks and trees. Sunlight played over the shimmering leaves, but he saw nothing unusual.

"Must have been imagining it," Frank said.

"I guess." Shaking himself, Joe continued down the trail. It curved sharply downward in front of a thick clump of bushes. Joe moved slowly, trying not to stumble on the loose rocks.

He was reaching out to steady himself on some branches when a sudden rustling right next to him made him jump. In the next instant someone shot toward him from behind the cover of leaves and branches. Joe did a double take when he saw Terry Brodsky's piercing blue eyes and thick, sandy hair. Up close, the guy was taller and even more muscular than he was in his photograph. And the expression on his chiseled face was all business.

"What—"

Joe's voice was cut off as Brodsky lashed his arm out and clamped it around Joe's throat in a choke hold. Out of the corner of his eye Joe saw his brother crouch as if he were ready to jump Brodsky.

"Don't move!" Brodsky growled.

Frank froze, his dark eyes flickering nervously. "He's got a knife, Joe," he whispered.

Joe had already caught sight of the flash of metal in Brodsky's free hand. A second later he felt the knife's sharp, pointy tip pressing against his throat.

"You two have caused me enough trouble," Brodsky said in a deadly serious voice. "So I'm putting an end to it—here and now."

Chapter
Sixteen

FRANK FLINCHED when he saw the cold, hard gleam in Terry Brodsky's eyes and the razor-sharp blade of the hunting knife he held to Joe's throat. The guy definitely meant business. Frank knew he wouldn't hesitate to use that knife. Judging by the fearful glint in his brother's eyes, Frank saw that Joe had come to the same conclusion.

"Go easy," Frank said, holding out his hands to show Brodsky he had no weapon. "Why don't you put that knife down so we can talk?"

"I'm doing the talking here," Brodsky said. But Frank noticed that he loosened his grip on Joe. "I'm going to make you two a deal. . . ."

Frank didn't feel that he and Joe had much bargaining power. "We're listening," he told Brodsky.

"You two fly back to wherever you came from

and forget all about me and the Phoenix missiles," Brodsky ordered.

"That'd be convenient for you, wouldn't it," Joe said, glaring at Brodsky out of the corner of his eye. "As if we'd just stand back and let you sell the missiles to Petronia."

"Joe—chill out, will you?"

Brodsky took a deep breath, then let it out in a rush. "You two have become a monumental pain—"

"I'll take that as a compliment," Joe cut in.

"Don't," Brodsky growled, his blue eyes flashing. "Look, you may not believe me, but I'm trying to protect you. You don't have a clue how dangerous the people you're messing with are."

Frank caught Joe's confused glance. The way Brodsky was talking, it was almost as if he wanted them to believe he didn't have anything to do with the stolen missiles. "What are you trying to say?" Frank asked.

"I'm just going to tell you this once. . . ." Brodsky stuck his hunting knife into a sheath that was attached to his belt. Then he looked Frank straight in the eye and said, "I did not steal the Phoenix missiles."

Frank had to stop himself from rolling his eyes. "How gullible do you think we are, Mr. Brodsky?" he asked. "You disappeared at the same time as the missiles *and* there's a photograph of you next to a truck filled with missiles."

"Photos can be doctored," Brodsky countered.

He ran a hand through his sandy hair. Frank was surprised to see that the expression in his eyes seemed to be sincere—and frustrated.

"If I had stolen those missiles, do you really think I'd bother to have this little chat with you?" Brodsky went on. "I'd have taken care of you two a long time ago."

Brodsky had a point, Frank had to admit. "So what are you saying, that someone *else* stole the missiles and set you up?" Frank asked.

"That's exactly what I'm saying," Brodsky said, fixing Frank with a steady gaze.

"But who? I mean, it would have to be someone with access to the missiles," Joe said.

Brodsky hesitated a moment before answering. "All you need to know about the person is that he's someone you shouldn't be messing with."

As Frank thought back over the last few days, Brodsky's story started making sense to him. "Joe and I couldn't figure out who would blow up those trucks at the Andromeda Palace," he said. "We didn't know anyone else besides us was trying to stop the sale of the missiles to Petronia."

"The less you two know, the better off you'll be," Brodsky told Frank and Joe. "Let's just say that blowing up those trucks would be one way of sending a message to the person who *did* steal the missiles, to let him know that he wouldn't get away with it."

"People could have been killed, you know," Joe pointed out.

"Someone who knew what he was doing could have waited until there wasn't anyone in the trucks, then detonated the explosives by remote control."

Frank couldn't believe it, but he was almost starting to like this guy. If it weren't for Brodsky, the Phoenix missiles might already be in Petronia. But there were still a few things that Brodsky hadn't explained. "If you're not mixed up with the stolen missiles, what were you doing in that deserted warehouse?" Frank asked.

"You guys are too curious for your own good," Brodsky muttered, shaking his head. "*If* someone called Constantine Shipping pretending to be the police, that person could probably find out all the information the company had on the trucks that were blown up," he went on. "Even if the information turns out to be bogus, it pays to be thorough."

So, Frank thought, Brodsky had been following clues on his own, trying to get to the person who had the Phoenix missiles. He must have gotten the phony address for K&B Imports from Constantine Shipping, just as Joe had.

Brodsky stood up, fixing first Frank, then Joe, with a deadly serious look. "The only reason I'm telling you this is because the two of you are in serious danger," he added.

"Tell me about it. We narrowly missed being

skewered by a fishing spear," Frank said. "What about Alexis Constantine? Did you kidnap her?"

Brodsky just stood there, frowning at them in stony silence.

"Why did you break into Constantine Shipping and tap into their communications lines?" Joe asked. "Who was that guy you were with in the truck? And what did you do with the money you took from him?"

"I don't have to explain myself to you two," Brodsky said. "But you should know one thing. If you two don't back off trying to get those missiles, we could all wind up dead."

He shot them a final warning look. Then, moving quickly and smoothly, he stepped off the trail and darted down the steep hill. Within seconds he disappeared among the trees.

"Weird," Joe muttered, staring into the lush gorge. "What do you think? Is he on the level?"

Frank wasn't sure what to make of what had just happened. "My gut feeling is that he's telling the truth," he said slowly. "But if he thinks we're going to back off this case . . ."

Joe grinned at him before finishing. "Then he doesn't know how the Hardy brothers operate!"

"So this is Chora Sfakion," Nancy said, late Sunday afternoon. She, Bess, and Petros were leaning against the railing of the *Island Princess,* looking toward the southern coast of Crete. A tiny seaside town was nestled into the hills.

Nancy spotted the white cross of a church, brilliant splashes of color from flowering bushes, and the smooth, pastel-colored walls of the houses, stores, and restaurants around the harbor.

"Too bad we didn't come up with any clues as to where Alexis is being held when we were in Chania," Bess said. "I hope we have better luck here."

Nancy felt the same way. They'd arrived at Chania late the previous afternoon and had spent the entire evening checking out hotels and tourist spots for any sign of the man with the tattoo who'd picked up the ransom money. They'd come up empty-handed, but when they returned to the yacht that night, Captain Costas gave them messages from Alexis's father. The Hardys had called to say that they were following a lead to Chora Sfakion. And since the Constantines' island, Kiros, wasn't far, Mr. Constantine and Petros had decided that the *Island Princess* would head there and wait.

"We have to stop here for provisions before continuing on to Kiros," Petros said. "I should be gone for an hour or so."

"Do you need any help? Bess and I could go with you," she offered. Since leaving Piraeus, she'd hardly let herself sleep. So far, Petros hadn't said or done anything suspicious, but if he was going somewhere, she wanted to go with him.

Petros shook his head. "I must take the speed-boat to a supply store at the edge of town," he said, nodding to the small motorboat that was stored on deck, next to the steering house. "There isn't enough room for all of us *plus* the supplies. Why don't you two enjoy yourselves, take a look around the town? It's really quite charming." He smiled, but his dark eyes didn't show any warmth.

Nancy didn't see how she could press the issue without making him too suspicious, so she just nodded and said, "Sounds good."

Ten minutes later the yacht was moored in the harbor and Captain Costas was helping Petros set the motorboat in the water. Soon after, Petros was buzzing away from them across the deep blue water.

Nancy and Bess started across the maze of docks toward the shore. "You think he's up to something funny?" Bess asked.

"I'm not sure, but there's nothing we can do to stop him now." Nancy watched as the speedboat disappeared around some rocks at the edge of the harbor. Then she turned resolutely toward the town. "We might as well look around. Maybe we'll run into Frank and Joe."

Bess pointed up toward a row of merchants' stalls located just beyond an outdoor café that overlooked the harbor. "Let's start over there."

"You're amazing, Bess. We haven't even gotten

off the docks yet, and you've already scoped out the shopping situation," Nancy teased.

"What can I say?" Bess said. "It's a natural talent."

The area right next to the harbor was a maze of pastel buildings with balconies, stairways, and walkways twisting in every direction. Brightly colored doors and shutters echoed the blues and greens of the sea. Wide-open ground-floor doorways revealed tiny shops crowded with fabric, jewelry, pottery, and local crops such as olives or honey.

Nancy was looking at some earrings that were on display when she heard Bess's breath catch in her throat. "Is that Theo?" Bess whispered.

Nancy caught a quick glimpse of a tall guy with curly dark hair up the street. He was bent over something, so she couldn't really see his face.

"Theo!" Bess called, starting toward him.

Nancy still couldn't see his face, but he definitely straightened up at the sound of Bess's voice. Instead of coming toward her and Bess, he walked quickly *away* from them, disappearing around the side of a building.

"That's weird," Bess murmured.

"I'll say," Nancy said, hurrying to the spot where the man had been standing. When she got there, she saw a small alleyway that twisted between buildings, rising up the hillside. A hunched-over, gray-haired man was walking toward them, leading a burro, but Nancy didn't see Theo anywhere.

"Nothing, huh?" Bess asked, catching up to her. She looked up the alleyway, then sighed. "I guess it wasn't Theo, after all."

"It *did* look an awful lot like him," Nancy said. "Maybe he's here with his aunt and uncle."

"But Theo wouldn't have run away from us like that," Bess said firmly.

"I guess not," Nancy agreed. It didn't make sense that he would be messed up with Alexis's kidnapping *or* the stolen missiles. But if that *was* Theo, then why had he run from them? And when clues brought her *and* the Hardys here to Crete, was it coincidence that Theo might have turned up at the same place?

Nancy shook herself. Maybe Bess was right and it wasn't even him. But somehow, she couldn't completely erase the doubt from her mind. . . .

"What are you doing, Frank?" Joe asked. "Trying to memorize the entire coastline between the Samaria Gorge and Chora Sfakion?"

He and Frank had finished their hike through the gorge an hour earlier, and now they were taking the ferry to Chora Sfakion. After hiking for over six hours *and* being in close quarters with a very sharp hunting knife, Joe was just trying to take it easy. But ever since their ferry had left the tiny coastal village where the gorge ended, Frank had been leaning against the railing with his eyes glued to the shore.

"Can't hurt," Frank murmured, without looking at Joe. "If Brodsky's in this area, then maybe the guy with the tattoo is, too."

"Or the Phoenix missiles." Joe leaned against the railing next to his brother. The terrain they were passing was mostly rocky, dry cliffs and scrub pine. But some dark indentations in the rock just above sea level caught his attention.

"Check it out," Joe said. "Are those caves?"

Frank gave a sober nod. "I was thinking the same thing. And look." He pointed to what had to be a wide cave. "I could swear I saw something move in there."

Joe peered at the cave. For a second he saw what might have been movement. "It's hard to tell from out here," he finally said. "But we could rent a speedboat or something after the ferry docks at Chora Sfakion and come back to take a closer look."

The town of Chora Sfakion was fairly small. There was a place right next to the dock where they were able to rent a speedboat. It seemed to take forever for the owner to gas up the boat and go through the paperwork. But finally Joe and Frank were pulling away from the dock. Joe was just steering the boat out of the harbor when he spotted a long white yacht with the name *Island*

Princess painted on its hull in gold letters. "Hey! That's the Constantines' yacht," he called to Frank.

Frank turned to look at the sleek boat. "I don't see anyone on board. We can stop for a visit when we get back," he said.

Joe poured on more speed, and they cruised out of sight of the harbor, retracing the route their ferry had taken. Soon the caves came into view. The sun was already setting, but there was just enough light for Joe to see the darker black of the caves against the rocky shoreline cliffs. "Which was the one where we saw that movement?"

Frank's eyes played watchfully over the coastline. "I think it was—" He broke off suddenly, "Joe! Stop the engine," he whispered urgently. "I see something!"

Joe immediately cut the power. They were still about a hundred yards from the shore. Looking at the cliffs, he spotted it, too—the silhouette of a man jumping onto a large, flat boat outside one of the caves. From what Joe could see, the boat was heavy in the water. "Looks like there's some serious cargo on there," he said in a low voice.

"Like maybe a half-dozen Phoenix missiles?" Frank guessed.

Joe concentrated on watching the boat. As it pulled slowly away from the cave, he heard the low droning of its motor. A hot wind whipped through Joe's hair. He felt the waves lapping against the outside of their own speedboat, and—

He realized that there was water *inside* their boat, too. "Hey!" Joe cried, jerking his soaking wet shoes from the boat's bottom. "We've sprung a leak!" He didn't know where the water was coming in, but four or five inches had already accumulated.

"I don't believe this," Frank said in a tight voice. He whipped his head around to gaze after the barge, which was heading out to sea in the darkening sky. "There's no way we can go after the barge now. We'll drown!"

Chapter

Seventeen

Joe slammed a fist against the side of the speedboat and let out a cry of frustration. "I don't believe this," he muttered. "The Phoenix missiles could be on that barge, and there's nothing we can do about it!"

He could see the low, flat boat's dark silhouette. It had pulled away from the shore and was heading toward open sea. Joe spotted the shape of a man on deck, but he was already little more than a black speck in the darkening sky.

"Uh, Joe?" Frank said. "I think we'd better stop worrying about that barge and figure out what we're going to do when *our* boat sinks."

"You're right!" Joe realized.

The leak was growing worse. His and Frank's feet were already covered with seawater, which was steadily rising to their knees. As Joe watched, the rear of the speedboat dipped below the surface. As if in slow motion, the boat sank lower and lower and the salty water closed in around him and Frank.

"We're going to have to swim to shore," Frank called out.

Joe started treading water, but his soaking jeans and T-shirt felt like lead and it was almost impossible to move freely. "It's nearly dark," he called to his brother, fighting back the worry that tightened his chest muscles. "And those cliffs are still a couple of hundred yards away."

"It's not like we have any choice. Come on, we'd better start swimming," Frank said. Joe didn't miss the grim expression on his brother's face, and he guessed what Frank was thinking— they were both strong swimmers, but if something did happen, no one could see them and come to their rescue.

Taking a deep breath, Joe launched himself with a powerful kick and started moving with a strong crawl. Before he'd gone more than a few strokes, he whacked into Frank's back.

"Hey!" Joe cried, stopping and shaking the water from his hair and eyes. "Why'd you—"

"Shhh!" Frank cut him off. "Do you see that?"

Frank was looking toward the shore. Even in the deepening twilight, Joe saw the tense set of his brother's face. When Joe followed Frank's gaze, he could just make out the silhouette of a motorboat coming toward them from one of the other caves.

"Another boat," Joe murmured, kicking his clothed legs clumsily to keep afloat. As the boat drew closer, the droning of its engine grew louder. "This could be trouble."

"Tell me about it," Frank agreed. "Whoever was on that barge could have friends in those caves who spotted us."

Peering into the darkness, Joe thought he saw a single person bent over the boat's outboard motor. He felt like a deer caught in the lights of an oncoming car—there was nothing he and Frank could do to outswim the boat.

When the speedboat was about ten feet from them, the driver cut the motor to a low rumble. Joe's entire body was instantly on red alert. For a few moments he heard nothing except the sounds he and Frank made treading water.

"Frank, Joe, are you all right?"

Joe could hardly believe it. He recognized that deep voice. "Brodsky?" he called back.

"You were expecting the tooth fairy?" Brodsky's voice came back. "You two okay?"

"We're fine," Frank told him.

As Brodsky edged his boat closer, Joe saw anger, worry, and frustration on his face. "I *told* you to keep out of this," Brodsky said sharply. "I ought to let you both drown."

"You wouldn't want to have that on your conscience, would you?" Joe shot back as he and Frank clambered into the boat.

"This is serious," Brodsky insisted. "The people you're dealing with can do a lot worse than punch a hole in the bottom of your boat, you know."

"Punch a hole," Frank echoed, staring at Brodsky in shock. "Are you trying to say that someone—"

"I'm not saying anything," Brodsky interrupted. He looked in the direction the barge had taken. "Now keep still," he ordered. "We'll be lucky if we can follow that boat without being spotted."

"We?" Frank asked Brodsky. "Does that mean we're working together now?"

"Apparently, that's the only way to keep you two out of trouble," Brodsky answered. He wasn't exactly rolling out the red carpet, but Joe did detect a slight smile on Brodsky's face.

"Aye aye, captain. Lead on," Joe said, making a smart salute.

"I wonder where Petros is?" Bess asked. She scanned the deck of the *Island Princess* as she and Nancy headed toward the yacht on the maze of harbor docks. "I don't see the speedboat."

"Me, either. And we've been gone over two hours. That's an hour longer than Petros said he'd be away," Nancy added. "Hello?" she called out. But the yacht seemed completely deserted.

"That's weird. Captain Costas isn't around, either," Bess said. "What's going on?"

Nancy shrugged. "I'm not sure, but . . ." Her

voice trailed off as she peered more closely at the yacht, which was shrouded in evening shadows.

"Uh-oh. You've got that look on your face," Bess said. "The one that usually means we're going to do something that could get us in trouble."

"Not if we're careful." Nancy headed up the ramp to the deck, with Bess following. "Let's nose around while no one else is here. I want to take a look in Petros's stateroom."

"What if he comes back?" Bess asked worriedly.

"We just have to hope that he doesn't." Nancy squared her shoulders and headed into the steering house, then down the narrow stairs that led belowdecks. She and Bess turned on lights as they hurried through the living room to the sleeping quarters at the rear of the yacht. During the overnight cruise from Athens to Crete, Nancy had learned that Petros's stateroom was at the far aft end of the yacht. When she tried his door, it was locked.

"Kind of makes you wonder what he's got to hide, doesn't it?" Bess said.

"Yup, and this lock isn't going to keep us from finding out." Nancy reached back to unclip the small barrette at the end of her French braid. She used the metal tip to work at the lock. Within a minute the door was open and she and Bess were inside. Nancy slipped her barrette into her shorts pocket and looked around.

The stateroom held a bed and an arrangement of wooden drawers built into its teak walls. The room wasn't large, but it felt spacious and comfortable.

"Petros sure is neat," Bess said, glancing around the spotless stateroom. "Where do we start?"

"I'll take the drawers," Nancy decided. "You start with the closet, okay?"

"Sure." Bess glanced out the narrow bank of windows that ran the width of the stateroom just above eye level. "But let's hurry!"

Three drawers were set into the wall next to the closet. Nancy quickly slid open the top one, which held two stacks of neatly folded shirts. Slipping her hand beneath one of the piles, she felt around.

"Nancy!" Bess called urgently. "Look!"

Nancy turned toward the closet. Bess was pulling something from the pocket of a navy suit jacket with brass buttons. Nancy gasped when she saw the thin gold chain dangling from Bess's hand. There was no mistaking the distinctive Greek key design.

"Alexis's necklace!" Nancy said, taking it from Bess. Her gaze flew to the end of the necklace, where the clasp should be. But the clasp had obviously been wrenched off. "So the clasp we found at Constantine Shipping *was* Alexis's."

Bess nodded excitedly. "Which means that

you were right about Petros, Nancy. He *did* kidnap Alexis. Otherwise, why would he have this?"

"Now that I think of it"—Nancy went to the closet and fingered the two brass buttons at the cuff of the blue sleeve—"I'm sure Petros was wearing this the day Alexis disappeared. I remember noticing those buttons." Dropping the sleeve, she turned toward the door. "Bess, we'd better call Mr. Constantine in Athens right away."

She had taken only half a step when she heard it—the sound of footsteps inside the yacht, moving rapidly toward the stateroom. "Oh, no," she said.

Before she could get to the door, it was blocked by Petros's compact body. "What are you doing in here?" he growled. "I should—" He broke off, staring at the necklace Nancy held.

Nancy fought off the fear that had overtaken her when she saw him. "We know you kidnapped Alexis," she accused, taking the offensive.

"Why'd you do it?" Bess asked. "Did you hate her *that* much for breaking off your engagement?"

For a long moment Petros stood without moving or saying anything. "I suppose it cannot hurt for you to know," he said at last.

Something about his tone made Nancy even more nervous than she had been. "What do you mean?" she asked him.

Petros gave a bitter shake of his head. "The engagement to Alexis was part of my plan, nothing more," he said. "When she broke it off, of course I was angry. She was getting in the way of my ambitions. . . ."

"Plan? Ambitions?" Nancy echoed.

"Christos Constantine has ruined my family!" Petros burst out, his face turning red. "Now I am going to make him pay."

Nancy tried to make sense of what Petros was saying. She remembered hearing something about his family from Yannis, the bouzouki player at the *rebetiko* club. It was a shot in the dark but . . . "Weren't your father and Mr. Constantine once business partners?" she asked.

"Yes. Until Christos decided that he wanted to have the business all for himself. He forced my father out of their partnership. It was a bitter loss. My father never recovered from it. He died when I was just a boy."

"Wow," Bess said. "That's awful."

Nancy wasn't sure it was the whole truth. "I thought that your father *wanted* to sell Christos his half of the business," she said, "because he was in poor health. Yannis never said anything about foul play. If your father blamed Christos, wouldn't his own uncle know about it?"

A dark, foreboding expression came into Petros's eyes. "Father would not blame Christos, but *I* do," he said in a low voice. "If Christos had treated my family fairly, half of the shipping company would still be ours today. For years I have been planning my revenge, working my way up in the business. I even let him believe that I loved his daughter. . . ."

While he spoke, Petros clenched and unclenched his fists, staring at a spot on the wall behind Nancy and Bess. He seemed to have forgotten that they were even there.

"But when he is least expecting it—bam!" Petros slammed a fist into his other palm. "I will destroy Christos from the inside. . . ."

"That's disgusting," Bess muttered.

Nancy had to agree. "I guess Alexis must have really ruined your plans when she broke off your engagement," she said to Petros. "Is that why you kidnapped her?"

For a split second Nancy thought she detected an uneasy glimmer in his dark eyes. But then it was gone. "Perhaps," he said mysteriously.

"Where did you take her?" Nancy pressed. "Was Alexis on the truck that went to Delphi?"

"Did you have any help?" Bess wanted to know. "Like maybe from Calliope Dalaras?"

It made sense, Nancy realized. After all, Dalaras was Mr. Constantine's enemy, too. But Petros just threw back his head and laughed. "You two don't have any idea of what is really going on, do you?"

His cocky tone irritated Nancy. But his words made her remember that there *were* a lot of big questions that still hadn't been answered. "If *you* kidnapped Alexis, then who was the man who picked up the ransom money?" she asked Petros.

Again Nancy caught the slightest hint of fear in his eyes, but he didn't say anything.

"We have reason to believe that he might be mixed up in transporting some missiles that were stolen from a U.S. military base near Athens," she went on. She crossed her arms over her chest. "You wouldn't happen to know anything about that, would you?" All of Nancy's instincts told her that he knew about the Phoenix missiles, but he remained stonily quiet.

After a short silence, Petros checked his watch and said curtly, "I have no time for this." He pulled a small revolver from the pocket of his blazer and aimed it at Nancy. "Come with me."

Nancy gulped. Before he revealed his weapon, she had hoped that she and Bess could overpower him. But now the situation had changed dramatically. She couldn't risk getting killed.

Nancy held her hands up, and she and Bess walked in front of Petros. He directed them to a metal door under the steering house, which he unlocked and opened. "Get in," he ordered.

A metal staircase went down to a dank, dark room that stank of diesel fuel. Nancy and Bess both stumbled as they climbed down the stairs to the metal floor. The only illumination came from the hallway light behind Petros. It filtered through the doorway, revealing greasy-looking machinery.

"In case you're wondering where Captain Costas is, I've given him a few days off," Petros called down. He gave Nancy and Bess a jeering smile and said, "Enjoy yourselves. This may be the last cruise you'll ever take."

Then the engine room door closed with a loud clang, leaving the girls in total darkness.

Chapter

Eighteen

NANCY?" Bess's whisper echoed in the darkness.

"Right here," Nancy assured her. With the door closed, the engine room was pitch-black. But she managed to make her way to the stairway and climb up to the door. She groped with her hands until she found the handle, then gave it a firm yank.

"It's locked," she told Bess, letting out a sigh. "We're stuck."

She heard a muffled thud, followed by a soft exclamation. Seconds later she felt Bess's hands brushing against her ankles. "Squeeze over, okay?" Bess asked in a small voice.

"Sure." Nancy made room for Bess to sit next to her on the metal stairs. Tucking her legs up, Nancy wrapped her arms around her knees and used them as a headrest. "We've got to figure out a way to get out of here," she whispered.

"But how?" Bess asked.

Nancy tried to focus on what to do, but the slight rocking of the yacht made her realize how tired she was. She'd hardly slept since leaving Piraeus. Even down in the smelly, dark engine room she couldn't keep her eyelids from closing heavily.

When Nancy awoke, the first thing she was aware of was the low rumble of the yacht's engine. Then she felt the boat dip and roll. She had to grab the metal railing to keep from losing her footing on the stairs. Her eyes had grown used to the shadows of the closed engine room. She could see Bess's silhouette next to her, slumped against the door.

"Bess, wake up," she said, shaking her. "I think the boat's moving."

"Huh . . . ?" Bess yawned and sat up groggily. "Where? What time is it?"

Now that Nancy looked around, she had the impression that it wasn't quite as black as it had been when Petros locked them up. "We're in the engine room, remember? I think it might be morning, but I'm not sure," she answered.

Bess leaned back against the door and let out a sigh. "Oh." She steadied herself on the metal stairs as the yacht took another dip. "Where's Petros taking us?" she whispered.

Nancy had just been asking herself that same question. "I don't know, but I have a feeling he's up to no good. Otherwise, why would he give Captain Costas time off?"

"Maybe he's taking us to wherever Alexis is," Bess suggested.

"Could be, but I think there's more going on than the kidnapping," Nancy said. "I'm not sure how everything fits together, but Petros knows something about the Phoenix missiles." She hit her hand against the metal railing in frustration. "We can't just sit here and do nothing," she went on. "We have to find a way to get out of here!"

"Except that there's only one way out," Bess pointed out. "And it's locked, remember?"

"I know, I know . . ." Nancy turned around and felt the damp, cold metal door until she found the lock. "It's a long shot, but if I could open Petros's stateroom with my barrette . . ."

"Maybe it'll work here, too!" Bess finished excitedly.

Nancy took the barrette from her shorts pocket. She played her fingers carefully over the lock. "There's a hole," she whispered. "If I can just work the lock with the metal tip . . ."

Biting her lower lip, she slid the tip of the barrette into the lock, delicately twisting and pushing. She could feel resistance, but she wasn't sure whether the slender bit of metal would hold against the lock. If she could just twist it a little more . . .

Holding her breath, she turned the barrette more forcefully. In the next few seconds the lock's bolt slid open with a heavy clunk.

"You did it!" Bess said in a triumphant whisper.

"Shhh!" Nancy cautioned. Very slowly, she pushed the door open and peeked out. Bright daylight streamed into the engine room, and Nancy had to blink a few times until her eyes got used to it. "I don't see Petros. He's probably up at the steering house," she whispered to Bess. "Come on."

She led the way to the stateroom that she and Bess had shared since leaving Piraeus. After carefully closing the door behind them, Nancy went over to the bank of windows just above eye level. "Let's try to figure out where we are," she murmured, climbing up on the bed that stretched along the wall beneath the window.

The yacht was approaching an island. A small harbor sat at the foot of some hills covered with trees and flowering bushes. Nancy spotted a dock and some low buildings. On the hill overlooking the harbor was the largest mansion she had ever seen. The modern house ran along the low cliff for hundreds of feet. Even from out on the water, Nancy spotted different terraces and a large pool. A flag on the dock had a yacht emblazoned on it that looked exactly like the *Island Princess*.

"That must be Kiros," Bess said. She had climbed onto the bed and was peeking out the window next to Nancy. "I wonder why Petros isn't stopping there?" she asked, nodding toward the harbor. "Doesn't that look like the main dock?"

"Definitely," Nancy answered. Sure enough, the yacht was bypassing the dock, heading around a rocky ledge that jutted out into the water. Nancy now saw nothing but deserted cliffs topped by a grove of shimmering, silver-green olive trees.

After about ten minutes Petros steered the yacht to a smaller dock that was nestled into a curve of sand at the foot of the cliffs. As soon as the yacht was moored, he set off on a small path that rose to the top of the cliffs.

"Let's follow him," Nancy said excitedly.

"Do you think he's holding Alexis captive here?" Bess asked. "On her family's own island?"

"Maybe," Nancy answered. "It's the one place Mr. Constantine would never think of looking. Someone else would have had to bring Alexis here, though. Maybe the guy with the tattoo."

As the two girls hurried through the yacht and climbed up to the steering house, Bess said, "Do you think Petros was telling the truth when he said he gave Captain Costas time off?" she asked. "What if Petros locked *him* up somewhere?"

"Good point." Nancy said.

The two girls softly called the captain's name, opening every door they came across, but they found no sign of him. When they emerged in the steering house, Nancy threw an urgent glance toward the path Petros had taken. He was just disappearing over the top of the cliff.

"We'll have to worry about Captain Costas later," she said, keeping a low voice. "Come on."

The two girls scrambled quickly up the path Petros had taken. Once they reached the top of the cliff, the path followed the outside edge of an olive grove, overlooking the deep blue sea. Petros was a few hundred feet ahead of them. She and Bess followed silently behind him.

After about ten minutes Petros followed the path down a zigzag route to another cove at the foot of the cliffs. "Hold up a sec," Nancy whispered. She paused next to an olive tree at the top of the cliffs.

The cove below was long and narrow and unusually lush. A large stand of trees filled everything except for the thinnest strip of sand at the water's edge. Petros was just disappearing beneath the thick cover of branches and leaves.

"Check it out," Nancy whispered, pointing to a long, low barge that was moored just off the beach. "That barge is protected by the cove. You wouldn't see it unless you were right on top of it."

"Do you think Alexis is there?" Bess wondered.

Nancy shrugged. "Let's go lower and see what else we see."

Keeping as low to the rocks as she could, she led the way down toward the cove. At first all she saw was the tops of the trees. But as the path descended more, she spotted movement. She pulled Bess behind a large rock at the foot of the cliff, then peeked around it to get a better look.

"It's Alexis!" she whispered.

Mr. Constantine's daughter was tied up against a tree trunk not more than fifteen feet away. She was still wearing the blousy white shirt she'd had on over her bathing suit the day she was kidnapped, but now it was dirty and wrinkled. Her small leather handbag lay on the ground next to her. Nancy could see the fear in Alexis's eyes as she looked up at Petros. Next to Petros was a squat, barrel-chested man whom Nancy recognized right away.

Bess drew in her breath sharply. "It's the guy with the tattoo!" she whispered to Nancy.

Nancy nodded, and pressed a finger to her lips.

Petros and the other man were less than twenty feet away. Even the slightest noise would alert them to their presence. Petros was speaking sharply to the other man in Greek. After a few moments the two of them walked away from Alexis. They got into a rowboat at the water's edge and rowed out to the barge. Nancy watched closely while they tied the rowboat to a metal ladder that led up to the deck. After climbing up, Petros went to a large tarp that covered something about waist-high. When he lifted up a corner of the tarp, Nancy's mouth dropped open.

"What do you know," she said. "The Phoenix missiles!"

Bess did a double take. "But . . . how did they get *here?* Where's Terry Brodsky?"

"We can worry about that later," Nancy said. *"After* we get Alexis out of here."

As she and Bess crept from behind the rock, Alexis's eyes widened in surprise. Nancy put a warning finger to her lips and darted the rest of the way to the young woman. Within seconds she and Bess had untied the ropes binding Alexis's hands and feet.

Nancy shot a worried glance over her shoulder, but Petros and the other man were still on the barge, and seemed to be arguing now.

"Come on! Let's get out of here!" Bess's urgent whisper brought Nancy's attention back to Alexis.

"We've got to get back to the *Island Princess* and contact your father, Alexis," Nancy whispered.

With a nod, Alexis ran for the path. Bess and Nancy took off right behind her. When they reached the top of the cliffs, Alexis stopped and turned to Nancy and Bess. "Thank you," she said, with a grateful smile. "How did you find me?"

"We're not out of trouble yet," Nancy reminded her. "Let's walk while we talk."

Alexis nodded, then moved quickly along the cliffside path ahead of Nancy and Bess.

"We found your necklace in Petros's stateroom," Bess said from behind Nancy. "He admitted that he kidnapped you."

"We're still not sure why, though," Nancy added. "At first we thought it might be to get back at you for breaking off your engagement. But now that we know he's involved with the stolen Phoenix missiles . . . Do you know anything about that?"

Alexis just shrugged helplessly as she moved ahead of Nancy. "I cannot tell you much," she said over her shoulder. "When Petros first kidnapped me at my father's warehouse, he hid me on a barge at the docks. The missiles were on the barge, and so was Dimitrios."

"Dimitrios?" Bess echoed. "He's the man with the tattoo on his arm, right?"

As Alexis nodded, a few strands of auburn hair shook free of the unkempt knot at the nape of her neck. "Petros and Dimitrios did not speak about the missiles when they were around me, but I heard them talking on the barge one time," she explained, moving nimbly around the edge of the olive grove. "They thought I was sleeping. From what I could tell, they are planning to sell the missiles to Petronia."

Nancy glanced out over the water, but she still couldn't see the *Island Princess*. "So *Petros* stole the missiles?" she said, trying to fit all the pieces of the puzzle together. "But how could he have gotten past security at a U.S. military base?"

"We don't know anything about Dimitrios," Bess said. "Maybe he worked at the military base and pulled the job from the inside? But that still wouldn't explain why Petros decided to get *you* mixed up in the whole thing, Alexis."

Alexis paused for a second, and Nancy had the impression she wanted to say something. But then Alexis moved quickly forward on the path again.

Nancy hurried to catch up. With so much going on, she had forgotten about suspecting that Alexis herself was hiding something. "Alexis, is there something you're not telling us?" she called ahead. "Something that would explain why you didn't want extra security after you were attacked on Spetses? And why you didn't want us asking any questions about that paper you found in your purse at the *rebetiko* club?"

Again Alexis stopped. She took a deep breath as she turned around to face Nancy and Bess. "There *is* something," she admitted, her eyes flashing with uncertainty. "It's about Terry and me."

"Terry? You mean, Terry Brodsky?" Nancy asked, staring at Alexis in surprise. "You two know each other?"

Nancy was sure she must have heard wrong, but Alexis nodded and declared simply, "We were in love."

"What!" Nancy and Bess both exclaimed at once. Nancy was reeling with shock. How was this possible?

Alexis stared out at the water. "I met him a year ago, when I was on vacation on Corfu. I thought he was a tourist, like me. That was what he told me. He said his name was Terry Halloway."

"You didn't know he was an undercover operative for the U.S. government?" Nancy asked gently. She was so caught up in the story that she forgot all about their urgency to get back to the yacht.

"All I knew or cared about was that we fell in love," Alexis said dreamily. "We spent a week together. And then, one day . . . poof!" She snapped her fingers. "He disappeared."

"Oh, no . . ." Bess said.

Alexis went on. "For a while I received small gifts—mementos of our time on Corfu."

"The napkin and postcard we found in your wallet?" Nancy guessed.

Alexis gave a slow nod. "There was never a note or even a name attached, but I knew Terry sent them," she said quietly. "But after a few weeks I stopped hearing from him altogether."

"That's *so* sad," Bess murmured.

"Yes," Alexis agreed. "I tried to get over Terry. I knew that it was my father's wish for Petros and me to marry, so I did not protest when Papa encouraged me to spend more time with Petros. I did not love him"—she stamped her foot on the chalky path and clenched her fists together angrily—"but I never would have guessed that he could do such terrible things to my father and me."

As she listened to the story, Nancy couldn't help feeling sorry for Alexis. But there were still so many unanswered questions. "Why did Brodsky drop out of sight?" she asked Alexis. "Did he steal the Phoenix missiles?"

"Never!" Alexis burst out. "Terry would never betray his country!"

Nancy wasn't sure what to say next. She didn't want to insult Alexis or hurt her feelings, but she couldn't help wondering if Alexis could really know Terry Brodsky that well after just one week.

"Terry dropped out of your life a year ago. A lot could have happened between then and now," she said gently.

Alexis shook her head firmly and said, "He's an honorable man. He tried to warn me that I might be in trouble. That note you saw me reading at the club—it was not a threat, as you feared. It was a note warning me that I might be in danger. That is why I ran out of the club. I was hoping I would see Terry."

"So *that's* why you didn't want Nancy and me to be your guests on the yacht," Bess said, snapping her fingers. "And why you didn't want extra security after that guy tried to get you when you were sunbathing in that cove at Spetses."

Alexis nodded. "I did not want to spoil any chance that I might have to see Terry. And I certainly did not want the authorities to find him."

Again Nancy found herself wondering how Alexis could be so sure that Terry *hadn't* stolen the missiles. "What did the warning say, exactly?" Nancy asked. As her gaze swept out over the water, she remembered how close they still were to Petros and Dimitrios. "Let's keep going," she urged Bess and Alexis.

Alexis nodded. After shooting a nervous glance back toward the cliff where she'd been held captive, she moved quickly forward on the path again. "The note said, 'Remember Corfu and trust your heart. Do not believe rumors. You are in danger from those who do not want me to catch them and reveal the truth. They know I will do anything for you.'"

"I still don't get it," Bess said, bringing up the rear. Nancy could hear the doubt in her voice. "How could Brodsky have put the note in your bag without being seen?"

"Terry could do it. Is he not a top undercover agent?" Alexis said. "I was not carrying my bag every second, and the club was crowded. If Terry was wearing a hat and sunglasses, there is no reason I or anyone else would recognize him."

Nancy followed Alexis in silence for a few moments, thinking. "'Do not believe rumors' . . ." she murmured, repeating the line from the note.

"He must be talking about the rumors that he stole the Phoenix missiles," Bess said. Nancy could hear her sneakers scraping on the path behind her. "Sounds like he's saying that someone *else* stole the missiles. The person who doesn't want Terry to 'reveal the truth.'"

"Petros and Dimitrios," Nancy supplied. "We *know* they're mixed up in the missiles. But there's something I don't get. Joe said there was evidence against Terry Brodsky, some photos, I think."

"Terry must have been set up. It is the only explanation," Alexis said firmly.

Nancy still wasn't convinced, but the more she thought about Alexis's argument, the more it made sense to her. "Terry's warning makes it sound as if he's trying to catch whoever stole the Phoenix missiles," she said slowly, trying to put her thoughts into words. "Do you think he'd go so far as to blow up a couple of trucks to make sure they couldn't be used to transport the missiles overland?"

"Whoa!" Bess said from behind Nancy. "If that's true, Petros and Dimitrios wouldn't have been very happy about it."

"That's what I'm getting at," Nancy said,

glancing down at her feet as they flew along the path. "If Petros and Dimitrios knew how much Alexis meant to Terry—"

"Everything!" Bess put in in a dreamy voice.

"—then that would explain why they kidnapped you," Nancy finished. "To force Terry to back off his private mission to catch them. They must have guessed that Terry wouldn't do anything to endanger your life. They probably intended to keep you until after the Phoenix missiles were delivered to Petronia. You were their insurance policy."

"That's sick," Bess said.

"Yes, but unfortunately I think that is exactly what happened," Alexis said sadly.

Everything was happening so fast. Alexis had answered a lot of questions, but there was still something that didn't make sense to Nancy. "I'm sorry, but I just don't see how Petros could be the mastermind behind this whole scheme," she told Alexis and Bess. "I mean, he's bitter and resentful, but I can't imagine his taking on a highly trained military operative. How would that help him to get revenge against your family, Alexis?"

"And how could he even know about you and Terry?" Bess asked from behind Nancy. "Could he have seen you two together on Corfu?"

Alexis slowed down to look back at Nancy, shaking her head. "He and my father were negotiating an important business deal in France.

And after Terry disappeared, I was so upset and embarrassed . . . I never told anyone about him, not even Papa."

"So, if Petros didn't know about you and Terry, it makes sense that someone *else* planned to steal the missiles and sell them illegally," Nancy said. "Someone who *did* know about you two. That person is the one who decided to use your relationship with Brodsky against him."

Her mind was working just as quickly as her feet as she examined every possibility. "Maybe Brodsky was on some kind of undercover mission," she suggested. "That would explain why he used a phony last name."

"And why he dropped out of sight so suddenly," Bess finished.

"Alexis, do you remember seeing anyone else with him on Corfu?" Nancy called ahead. "Anyone he mentioned as a friend or business acquaintance?"

Alexis stopped on the path and stared out over the water, her brow furrowed in concentration. "No one," she finally answered. She reached into her bag for her wallet, then pulled out the folded paper napkin and postcard. "These are from the café where Terry and I met. I am sure no one was with him then."

She handed the napkin and postcard over to Nancy, then unzipped the wallet's change purse. "He sent me this amulet, too," she continued. "It comes from a small village near Corfu town. Terry and I drove there one afternoon."

Nancy stared at the distinctive yellow, blue, and white geometric design on the amulet. "That looks so familiar," she murmured.

"These are made only in that one small village," Alexis explained. She pointed to the blue triangle that dominated the tiny amulet. "That represents the spring where villagers blessed their animals in ancient times. I do not think that the design is sold anywhere else—"

"We *have* seen it before," Bess interrupted excitedly. "Theo had one, remember? He was wearing it when we went to Delphi."

"That's right!" Nancy said, frowning. "But he told us he bought it at the market in Athens. . . ."

"That is very unlikely," Alexis insisted. "The artisan told us that very few of the amulets are made. They are not a big tourist item."

"But why would Theo lie?" Bess asked.

Just then Nancy caught sight of a movement on the path ahead of Alexis. Her whole body stiffened when she saw Theo's curly dark hair and round face appear from around a bend in the path.

"Theo!" Bess exclaimed. "What are *you* doing here?"

Theo frowned when he saw them. In answer to Bess's question, he raised a pistol and pointed it straight at the girls.

Chapter

Nineteen

FRANK CROUCHED behind a rocky ledge that was just out of sight of the cove where the Phoenix missiles were being stored. Joe and Terry Brodsky were kneeling right next to him.

"How much longer do we have to wait here?" Joe whispered.

"Until I say we move," Brodsky answered.

Joe nodded. The evening before, they had tailed the barge in Brodsky's speedboat. From a distance, they'd seen the barge weigh anchor in this deserted cove. They'd stowed their speedboat between two high rocks farther along the coast, then made their way back on foot. The three of them had been waiting and watching ever since. So far, what they'd seen was anything but boring.

He and Joe had been right about the barge. The Phoenix missiles were on board, underneath a tarp. Frank had spotted them when the stocky man with the tattoo lifted the tarp to check the cargo. Frank had been surprised to learn that Alexis was on the barge, too. The stocky man had ferried her to shore the night before and tied her up next to a tree. At first the man had appeared to be on his own. Frank and Joe were both in favor of jumping him, but Brodsky had absolutely refused. He was waiting for something, but he wouldn't say what.

So, here they were, half a day later, still on the rocky ledge. Not that there wasn't plenty going on. First Petros had appeared. Frank still didn't know how he fit into the plan, but since the missiles were being stored on Kiros, obviously he was involved. For the last half hour Petros and the man with the tattoo had been arguing about something on the barge. They hadn't even noticed Nancy and Bess sneaking down to free Alexis.

Frank had been totally surprised to see the girls. "I wonder when they're going to figure out that Alexis is gone. And what Petros and the other guy plan to do with the missiles." He still hadn't seen any sign of Josef Kozani or Sofia. . . .

"Uh-oh." Brodsky's whisper broke into Frank's thoughts. "Looks like trouble."

Glancing back at the cove, Frank spotted Nancy, Bess, and Alexis climbing back down to the cove from the cliff. There was a man behind them. At first all Frank saw was the gun he held.

Then his face came into view, and Frank did a double take.

"Theo Papandreou?" Frank said, surprised.

"For a couple of crack detectives, you've got a lot to learn," Brodsky whispered, keeping his eyes on the cove. "You wanted to know who set me up. Well, now you have your answer."

"He's the undercover operative?" Frank asked. It was hard to believe—Theo had seemed a harmless student. But when Frank saw the way he barked out something in Greek to Petros and the other man on the barge, he realized there was more to Theo than he and Joe had assumed.

Petros and the short, barrel-chested man appeared surprised to see the three girls with Theo. They quickly climbed off the barge and started to row back to shore. Theo kept up a stream of angry words as he herded the girls toward the water.

"Time to move," Brodsky whispered. "Our best chance is to split up and move in from different directions."

Frank quickly gauged the layout of the cove. "I can make my way over to the other side of the cave to block the path," Frank whispered.

"Good," Brodsky said, nodding. "I'll swim out to the barge. Joe, you stay here and cover this end. Don't do anything until I give a signal."

Nancy, Bess, and Alexis huddled at the edge of the cove's narrow beach with their hands in the air. Theo was next to them, yelling at Petros and Dimitrios in Greek, but he kept his gun leveled at the girls. Nancy didn't dare make a move.

When the rowboat reached the sandy cove, Petros climbed out. He glared at Nancy and Bess, but didn't say anything to them. "Petros and Dimitrios have failed to keep you out of trouble," Theo said, switching to English. "I am afraid that now we must resort to a solution that is more permanent. A one-way boat ride to the bottom of the sea, perhaps."

Nancy tried to think of something, *anything,* to distract Theo until she could come up with a way out of the mess they were in. "So, *you're* the mastermind of this operation, huh," she said to Theo, trying to sound impressed. "You really had us fooled."

"That was the idea," Theo said. Nancy winced as she felt the barrel of his gun jab into the small of her back. "You three, into the rowboat," he ordered.

Apparently, he wasn't going to be easily fooled. Dimitrios and Petros shoved Nancy, Alexis, and Bess into the rowboat, which rested on the sand at the water's edge. Theo made the three girls sit down, while Dimitrios fetched the rope that had bound Alexis. Then Theo and Petros used the rope to tie their hands behind their backs.

"You just pretended to like me, didn't you?" Bess blurted out.

"Sorry," he said in a voice that didn't sound at all apologetic. "What can I say? It was convenient to flirt with a cute girl who happened to be sitting next to Alexis Constantine's table."

Alexis glared at Theo. "You set Terry up," she accused. "You planted evidence so that people would think *he* stole the Phoenix missiles."

Theo gave them a long look before saying anything more. "What if I did? It's not as if you three can do anything about it," he scoffed. "Terry and I were both in on some secret talks with the Petronians that came before the official negotiations with U.S. diplomats. When funding fell through, the Petronian government made it clear that it would still be interested in an *un*official deal to buy U.S. military technology . . . *and* that it'd pay top dollar. Since we were the ones the Petronians had dealt with covertly, I guess they figured that we were the likeliest people to help out. Terry was too much of a Boy Scout to go along."

"So you framed him," Nancy cut in, shaking her head in disgust. "You must have planted the photograph that implicated him."

Theo gave an impressed nod. "It was a composite of two photos. One showed *me* with the missiles. The other was of Brodsky. I used computer enhancement to place Brodsky's face on the photo of my body."

"But you must have dropped out of sight after

the missiles were stolen, too. *And* you were in on the first secret talks with Petronia," Bess pointed out. "Wouldn't that make you a suspect, as well?"

"As far as central command knows, I'm on a mission in Romania right now," Theo said with a shrug. "Naturally, I could not move the Phoenix missiles by myself. Dimitrios and some of his associates—men who were my informants over the years—helped. We knew the police would be watching the Petronian border, so we arranged a rendezvous with a barge that Petros provided. Then the barge was moved to the Constantine Shipping docks to sit until the heat died down a little."

"With so many ships coming through our docks each day, who would notice one small barge?" Petros said proudly.

"That still doesn't explain why *you* weren't suspected, Theo," Nancy said.

"While the missiles sat at Constantine Shipping, I went to Romania to put in an appearance there and make everyone believe that I was working on my assignment. And it is always possible to pay the right people in order to have an alibi for the time the missiles were taken." Theo gave Nancy, Bess, and Alexis a smug smile. "After a few days I left to return here. I called to check in with my contact at central command, pretending that I am still in Romania. Central command is in the habit of giving undercover agents a lot of freedom, so they don't question me."

Nancy couldn't believe how arrogant and twisted Theo was. Just listening to him made her skin crawl.

"I hoped the military police would pick up Brodsky after I sent that photograph to central command. Unfortunately, Brodsky managed to elude them," Theo went on. He shook his head in annoyance. "If it weren't for him, my plan to truck the missiles to Petronia from Athens would have been carried out several days ago."

"So Brodsky *did* blow up those trucks at the Andromeda Palace," Nancy murmured. "That must be when you decided to kidnap Alexis. First you attacked her at Spetses—"

Theo nodded. "Petros was thoughtful enough to find out from Mr. Constantine where he planned on taking Alexis and her guests. Naturally, he passed the information along to me."

"*You* were the one who screwed things up that day," Petros said to Theo. "I had to take care of Alexis myself back at Constantine Shipping. There is a small storage shed right next to the warehouse. I hid Alexis there, then told security that I had already checked it, so that they would not."

"That's right," Nancy said, thinking back. "I remember seeing a shed outside that room Alexis liked to use." More pieces of the puzzle were falling into place. "Then you encouraged Bess and me to go to Delphi, to throw us off your trail. And when you told Theo, he suddenly found the time to get away from his aunt and uncle to come with us." Turning to Theo, she asked, "Why did you bother? You knew the trip to Delphi was a wild-goose chase."

"That was the fun of it," Theo answered, an evil smile twisting his lips. "Besides, your snooping around looking for Alexis was getting to be a pain. I figured if I could find a way to get you out of the way permanently, so much the better for me."

"Your plan almost worked, too, when you pushed that statue," Bess said, twisting around in the rowboat to look at him. "But, Theo, how did you even know about Terry and Alexis? You must have been with him on that mission at Corfu. That's where you got that amulet, the same one Alexis has."

"Very good," he answered, nodding. "Give the lady a prize."

Nancy couldn't believe how smug he was. He had betrayed his government and was about to kill three innocent people, all for money. It made her furious that he was actually proud of himself.

Petros and Dimitrios had disappeared beneath the trees again. When they returned, they were carrying a heavy canvas bag. Nancy gasped when

Petros took out a bundle of dynamite and a timer. She heard Alexis draw in her breath and exclaim under her breath in Greek.

"Theo, you can't!" Bess wailed.

"Just watch me," he said, his voice steely and cold.

Nancy looked around. Don't kid yourself, she thought. No one is going to come to our rescue.

Letting out a sigh, Nancy shifted her position to ease the rubbing of the rope against her wrists. That was when she saw it—something moving off to her left at the far end of the cove. Taking a second glance, Nancy spotted Joe Hardy's familiar blond head.

Yes! And if Joe was here, Frank was bound to be somewhere nearby. Nancy felt a renewed sense of hope. If she could just work her hands free of the rope . . .

Nancy gulped as Petros and Dimitrios began attaching the explosives and timer to the underside of the rowboat's rear bench. She had to keep them and Theo occupied so that they wouldn't spot the Hardys. "There's one thing I still don't undertand," she said, turning to Petros. "How did *you* get mixed up in all of this?"

"You are nothing but a snake, Petros!" Alexis spat out, glaring at him.

"I will be a very rich snake, after the Phoenix missiles are delivered to Petronia," Petros told her. Then, to Nancy, he said, "I was first approached by Theo's associate, Dimitrios. His language was vague, but I understood that there was a lot of money to be made if I would agree to arrange for two trucks to transport some illegal cargo. Naturally, I agreed."

"Naturally," Bess echoed, rolling her eyes.

"I covered my tracks by writing a false name and address in the log book," Petros continued. "Josef Kozani has a certain . . . reputation in the international community."

"You mean, he's been accused of trafficking in illegal weapons," Nancy stated bluntly. "So the authorities suspected him, instead of you and Theo."

For the last few minutes she had been twisting her hands, trying to loosen the rope. It had the slightest bit of give. Slowly and steadily she was trying to work the rope down over her knuckles. . . .

"You must have been only too happy to kidnap Alexis," she said to Petros. "It was another way to get revenge against the Constantines, wasn't it?"

Petros said nothing, but the bitter look he gave Alexis told Nancy that she was right.

"After the explosion, we knew the authorities would be watching the Petronian border with extra care," Theo explained. "And we knew we could not allow the barge with the missiles to remain at the Constantine Shipping docks for long. Even with Petros overseeing things and making sure no one went aboard the barge, it was too risky. Petros was kind enough to offer to store the missiles here on Kiros."

"So if the missiles were discovered, then my father would stand to get in trouble with the authorities," Alexis said bitterly. "That is exactly what you wanted, isn't it, Petros?"

Petros finished setting the timer, then straightened up and stepped from the rowboat. "Yes," he answered. "And today, Christos will lose his daughter, just as I lost my father."

No! Nancy wanted to scream. The rope was still around her hands. She'd managed to loosen it the slightest bit, but it still cut into her skin just above her knuckles.

Theo, Petros, and Dimitrios all grabbed the sides of the rowboat and began dragging it into the water. Nancy glanced up the shoreline in time to see Joe jump lightly up and over the rocks. He moved stealthily toward them.

Nancy tried to catch Alexis's and Bess's eyes to warn them to be quiet. But before she could, Alexis drew in a breath as she spotted Joe.

"What?" Theo shot a quick glance at Alexis, then straightened up and whirled around. Joe was still about twenty feet away. Before he could make another move, Theo's gun hand shot out, and he pointed the pistol at Joe's head.

"Freeze!" Theo growled.

Joe stopped short and raised his arms in the air. Nancy saw the frustration in his eyes as Petros ran over and twisted his arms behind his back.

Uh-oh, Nancy thought. Now we're *all* sunk!

Chapter

Twenty

FRANK WATCHED in dismay as Theo Papandreou and Petros Apollonios closed in on his brother. Frank had just found a hiding place behind a rock, at the bottom of the cliffside path, when Joe jumped down to the beach. Brodsky hadn't given a signal yet, but Frank knew why his brother had made his move. If he hadn't, Nancy, Bess, and Alexis would already be floating out to sea with those explosives.

What are we going to do now? Frank wondered.

On the beach, Petros was still holding Joe. The stocky man was keeping guard over the rowboat, while Theo slowly scanned the cove. Frank ducked quickly behind the rock and counted to ten before peeking out again. He glanced toward the water, searching for Brodsky. It took him a moment before he spotted Brodsky's head about ten yards from the shore.

Theo turned to Joe and said angrily, "Where's your brother?"

Joe struggled against Petros, who held his arms behind his back. "What makes you think *both* of us escaped when our boat sank?" he asked.

Frank could see that Theo wasn't buying Joe's story. He and Brodsky were going to have to move fast if they were to have any chance of catching Theo and his pals off guard.

Taking a deep breath, Frank bolted from behind the rock and ran to the nearest tree. When he peered toward the shore again, he saw Nancy give the slightest shake of her shoulders. Seconds later her eyes widened as she saw him. She lifted her hands up just high enough so that he could see them, then dropped them behind her back again.

Way to go! Frank thought, grinning. She'd managed to get free of the rope. That definitely increased their odds of subduing Theo.

Seeing Theo turn back to the rowboat, Frank darted to a thick tree trunk even closer to the open beach. He was just about fifteen yards from the rowboat now.

"Quick! Let's get rid of this crew," Theo ordered. While Petros shoved Joe toward the boat, Theo grabbed the side of the rowboat with one hand. He and the stocky man pulled it the last few feet to the water.

Out at sea, Frank saw Brodsky hold his thumb up above the water. That was it—the signal! A split second later Brodsky's head disappeared below the surface.

Frank jumped out from behind the tree and raced toward the rowboat with a rebel yell. Theo and Dimitrios both stopped pulling the boat and whirled around. Before Theo could lift his revolver, Frank made a running dive for his gun hand. At the same time, Joe dug his elbow into Petros's gut, knocking him off balance. Nancy leaped from the rowboat and hit the stocky guy in the solar plexus with a judo kick.

Frank latched onto Theo's wrist and the two of them flew into the water next to the rowboat. Frank's head went under. He could feel himself losing his grip on Theo's wrist.

Suddenly Frank felt another hand close around Theo's arm. Frank came up, sputtering, in time to see Brodsky wrap an arm around Theo's throat in a choke hold. Brodsky's other hand held Theo's wrist. Frank reached out and plucked the revolver from Theo.

"I'll take that," he said, grinning.

Looking over his shoulder, Frank saw that Joe had Petros facedown on the sand. The stocky man still seemed to be catching his breath. He was sitting in the shallow water, with Nancy standing over him.

Frank waded over to her and trained the gun

on the stocky man. "I'll take over here," he offered.

"Nancy—the dynamite!" Bess called from the rowboat in a high voice.

In seconds Nancy was bent over the bench where the explosives and timer were. Frank saw the look of concentration on her face as she reached for the wires. There were two of them, leading from the timer to the dynamite. She traced them both with her finger, then went to work unfastening one. Frank hardly let himself breathe. One wrong move . . .

"It's defused," Nancy called out. She let out a long sigh, then went to work on the rope that bound Bess and Alexis. "We're safe."

"I can't eat another bite," Nancy said breathlessly, the following night.

"That makes two of us," Frank agreed. "Christos Constantine really knows how to throw a party. This is the ultimate Greek shindig."

Nancy wasn't about to argue with him. The two of them were sitting at a long table on a terrace outside the Constantines' mansion on Kiros. Looking down the table, Nancy saw Bess, Joe, Alexis, Terry Brodsky, and more food than Nancy could eat in a lifetime.

The police had taken Petros, Theo, and Dimitrios into custody, and U.S. military officials were overseeing the return of the Phoenix missiles to the military base near Athens. As soon as Christos had heard that Alexis was safe and sound, he'd flown down to Kiros. He'd insisted that Terry Brodsky and the teens stay on as his guests, and arranged a huge outdoor celebration at his seaside mansion. Paper lanterns waved in the breeze. A pig was roasting in a huge pit overlooking the cliffs, and musicians were just warming up beneath a small tent.

"Captain Costas sure was surprised when he returned here after taking the time off that Petros gave him," Bess spoke up from Frank's other side. She nodded toward the tanned, bearded captain, who was standing next to the musicians.

"No kidding," Nancy said. "He didn't have any idea that Petros had kidnapped Alexis *or* that half a dozen stolen, high-tech missiles had been right here on Kiros."

She, Frank, and Bess all turned as Christos Constantine came out of the mansion, followed by Calliope Dalaras. Frank leaned close to Nancy and whispered, "When did those two get to be so chummy? I thought they were mortal enemies."

"Not anymore," Nancy answered. She smiled as the two older people sat down next to Alexis and Terry Brodsky and began talking amiably together. "Apparently, Calliope came by the shipping office to yell at Christos because Bess and I followed her at Delphi. When she heard about Alexis being kidnapped, she totally changed her tune. She offered to help him out any way she could. Christos really appreciated her support."

"And Calliope *was* just at Delphi to drum up business, like the curator told Theo and me," Bess said.

Just then Christos stood up and tapped a spoon against his glass. "I would like to make a toast to the people who brought my Alexis safely back to me." He smiled down the table at Nancy, Frank, Joe, and Bess.

"Hey, we're just glad Theo, Petros, and Dimitrios are behind bars," Joe spoke up.

"I'm sorry about Petros, Papa," Alexis added gently. "I know that he was just like a son to you."

Christos frowned darkly, then shook himself. "He was a traitor. I do not wish to speak any more about him. Tonight, we are celebrating. I have my daughter back, and I have my million U.S. dollars as well."

Nancy was glad Christos had gotten the money back. She'd found out from Terry Brodsky that he'd stored the briefcase in a bus station locker after taking it from Dimitrios at the monastery of Daphni. He'd mailed the key to Christos, along with instructions on where to recover the briefcase.

"Not only that, but the police were able to pick Sofia up in Chora Sfakion," Frank said.

"Dimitrios spilled the beans about where to find her. I guess he figured that he might get a lighter sentence if he cooperated."

Bess shook her head in amazement. "I still can't believe she was overseeing the deal to buy the Phoenix missiles for Petronia. Who would ever guess that someone as young as she is could be mixed up in something so illegal?"

"That's the whole idea," Joe said. "Her uncle had been involved with the official talks with the U.S. But no one would suspect a girl like Sofia of trafficking in stolen high-tech weapons." He gave a wry shake of his head. "I know *I* didn't."

"What about Kozani?" Bess asked. "Was he involved?"

Frank shook his head. "Apparently not. I spoke to the Gray Man this morning. He suspects that Kozani came to Athens hoping to get a piece of the action. That's why he met Sofia at that café."

"But she'd already made a deal with Theo," Joe went on, "so Kozani was left out in the cold."

"Please, I have one more announcement to make," Christos was saying.

Looking toward the other end of the table, Nancy saw that he was smiling tenderly at Alexis. "I would like to make a toast to my daughter—and her new fiancé, Terry Brodsky."

Everyone started clapping and hooting. Brodsky nodded with embarrassment. Nancy had the feeling that he wasn't comfortable being the center of attention.

"You'd better get ready for a life full of intrigue, Alexis," Bess said, her blue eyes sparkling. "You're going to be married to a secret agent."

Alexis laughed, reaching out to take Terry's hand. "Actually, Terry has decided to give up undercover work."

"I've learned the hard way that it can be too dangerous for the people I love," Brodsky added gruffly.

As he leaned over to kiss Alexis, Bess let out a sigh. "That is *so* romantic," she said.

"I'm sorry things didn't work out as well for you, Bess," Nancy said sympathetically.

"Don't worry about me. It's not as if I've given up on love," Bess said, grinning. She raised her glass and stared out at the shimmering blue sea. "As far as I'm concerned, Greece is still one of the most romantic places on the planet."